Date: 5/10/16

FIC SILK WHITE
Silk White.
Tears of a hustler 6 : the
return of the Wolf /

TEARS OF A HUSTLER 6

The Return of the Wolf

A novel

SILK WHITE

Good2Go Publishing

This novel is a work of fiction. All the characters, organizations, establishments, and events portrayed in this novel are either product of the author's imagination or are fiction.

Published by:
GOOD2GO PUBLISHING
7311 W. Glass Lane
Laveen, AZ 85339
www.good2gopublishing.com
Twitter @good2gobooks
G2G@good2gopublishing.com
Facebook.com/good2gopublishing
ThirdLane Marketing: Brian James
Brian@good2gopublishing.com

Cover design: Davida Baldwin
Editor: Kesha Buckhana
ISBN: 9781943686889

BOOKS BY THIS AUTHOR

Married To Da Streets

Never Be The Same

Stranded

Tears of a Hustler

Tears of a Hustler 2

Tears of a Hustler 3

Tears of a Hustler 4

Tears of a Hustler 5

Tears of a Hustler 6

Teflon Queen

Teflon Queen 2

Teflon Queen 3

Time Is Money *(An Anthony Stone Novel)*

Acknowledgments

To you reading this right now. Thank you for stepping inside the bookstore, stopping by the library, or downloading a copy of Tears of a Hustler 6. I hope you have enjoyed this read from top to bottom. My goal is to get better and better with each story. I want to thank everyone for all their love and support. It is definitely appreciated!

Now without further ado Ladies and Gentleman, I give you **"Tears of a Hustler 6"**. ENJOY!!!

$iLK WHitE

PROLOGUE
The Return of the Wolf

J acob sat in a beat up chair with his feet kicked up on an old looking raggedy table. A blunt hung from between his lips and in his hand was a Hip Hop Weekly magazine. Today, Jacob was feeling good. He had just gotten promoted from doing hand to hand transactions to running a trap house and to say that he was happy about it was an understatement. He sat back smoking a blunt and reading his magazine while one of his workers did all the work. Jacob had never met Pauleena personally, but he was glad to be a part of her organization. To be down with a major movement like hers in the drug game held a lot of weight, not to mention Pauleena had the best product in the city so the money came quick and easy.

Jacob sat reading an article about Jay-Z when he heard a loud knock at the door. The fiends came like clockwork. At least every two minutes there would be a customer at the door looking to cop some of the potent product.

"Yo go take care of that!" Jacob yelled out to a worker.

"Bitch ass nigga stay yelling at somebody like he a boss! Fuck outta here!" the worker said to himself as he walked to the door and snatched it open with an attitude. On the other side of

the door stood a woman, her clothes were filthy and her hair was matted down all across her head.

"What you need?" the worker barked.

"I need four dubs, but I don't have any money," the woman said looking down at the young man's crotch. "Why don't you hook a sister up?"

"Bitch!" the worker barked. "If you ain't got no money then you just assed the fuck out!" He went to slam the door in the crack head bitch face, but she quickly stuck her boot in the door before it closed.

"Wait I got something better than money," she said reaching down in her back pocket.

"The fuck you got that's better than money!" the worker asked.

"This!" the woman said as she pulled a .380 from her back pocket. She jammed the gun in the pit of the workers stomach and pulled the trigger twice back to back.

POW! POW!

The sound of the two shots ringing out startled Jacob. It almost caused him to fall out of his chair. *"What the fuck?"* he said to himself. He was just about to get up and go grab the backup 9mm that rested under the sofa, when a crack head looking chick appeared in the doorway pointing a gun at his head.

"Listen bitch!" Jacob began with his hands raised in surrender. "I realize that you might be high and all that, but your best bet would to be to turn around and go on about your business," he warned.

Without warning, the woman backed slapped him across his face with the hammer knocking him out of his chair and down to the filthy floor. Before Jacob could utter another word he heard the loud roar of a machine gun being fired coming from outside. That could only mean that whoever the crack head woman's partner was, had just shot up the two look outs that stood posted up outside. Seconds later Jacob saw a man in all black walk around the corner holding a Mac-10 in his hand. Jacob looked up into the man's face and almost shitted on himself.

Wolf stepped around the corner and looked down at the man who was in charge. "Thanks baby you did a good job," he said leaning over and kissing Ivy on the lips. They had been up all morning fixing her up so she could pull off the crack head imitation.

"You already know," Ivy replied with her gun still trained on Jacob.

"Wolf, man that shit going on between you and Pauleena ain't got shit to do with me. I'm just out here trying to get my money," Jacob pleaded.

"I'm going to make this real simple for you," Wolf said speaking in an even tone. "Tell me where I can find Pauleena and you get to keep your life."

"I'm just a peon in this shit fam," Jacob said. "I'm still working my way up the food chain. I've never even seen Pauleena before in my life."

"Either you can help me or you can't," Wolf said. He had no time to be playing games. Pauleena had taken the life of his daughter Sunshine and anybody affiliated with her had to pay for what she'd done.

Behind Wolf and Ivy, another man crept from upstairs when he heard the shots ring out. He eased his way downstairs and made eye contact with Jacob, nodding his head as if to say *"I got you."* He then made a move for the sofa where the backup gun was.

Jacob made eye contact with his fellow member who worked in the trap house along with him and tried to hold Wolf's attention long enough so his partner could reach the gun that was stashed in the sofa. "Listen, I can try and make a few calls and see who knows what, that's the best I can do, but you have to promise not to kill me," he said.

Out the corner of his eye, Wolf saw movement. He spun around and filled the man that stood before him with bullets. The man's body jerked as if he was having a seizure and then dropped down to the floor.

"Fuck it!" Jacob hopped up to his feet taking advantage of the situation. He charged Ivy, hitting her hard, and lifting her off her feet. The two went crashing down to the floor hard. Wolf thought about getting the man up off of Ivy, but decided to stand back and see how Ivy handled herself under pressure. She had begged him to let her come along with him and help kill Pauleena, now it was her turn to show and prove that she belonged.

Ivy tussled with Jacob for a few seconds before she shot him in the leg. She quickly stood to her feet and stood over Jacob with the .380 pointed down at his head. "Where the fuck can we find Pauleena at?"

"I swear on my kids, I don't know where Pauleena is," Jacobs pleaded. "Come on don't do this I got kids."

"Fuck you and your kids!" Ivy snapped and then pulled the trigger shutting Jacob's lights out for good.

TEARS OF A HUSTLER 6
The Return of The Wolf

CHAPTER 1

"The Return of the Wolf"

R andy sat at the kitchen table counting stack after stack of money. His job was to go around to every trap house and drug spot that Pauleena ran and collect all of the money at the end of each and every night. Then at the end of the week he was to report to Prince and give him the money that he collected. This may have seemed like an easy job, but the truth was this job was the most dangerous job of them all. If any money was to come up missing or be misplaced, Prince would automatically believe that Randy was stealing and kill him. God forbid if he got robbed, Prince would probably still think he was lying and kill him, so with the type of job that Randy had he had to be mistake proof. One mistake could and would cause him his life.

After counting up all the money, Randy neatly stacked the money in a large duffle bag, leaned back, and breathed a sigh of relief. He had learned firsthand that counting large sums of cash was more exhausting than working a regular 9 to 5.

"Damn so after you count all that money you just gotta give it to somebody?" Tiffany huffed from the sofa. She was a part-time stripper whose career had seen its better days. Tiffany and Randy had been living together for the past six months and they fought almost every chance they got mostly over the smallest and stupidest things.

"Why you always gotta say some dumb shit?" Randy said shaking his head.

"What?" Tiffany barked. "If you were smart you would think about taking me and running away with all that money." Randy sighed loudly. Every time it was time for him to turn in the money, Tiffany always tried to talk him into running away with the money. Little did she know, but if Randy ever did decide to run off with the money, Tiffany would be the last person he took with him. "Fuck is you always worrying about what I'm doing? Shouldn't you be in the club twerking or popping that pussy or something?"

"Oh no the fuck you didn't!" Tiffany snapped. "Listen let me explain something to you. You not going to talk to me the way you talk to all of your other little side bitches cause trust and believe I'm not the one. We'll be up in this motherfucker fighting!" she said meaning every word of it.

"Shut up," Randy said as he got up and grabbed the duffle bag that was filled with cash. "I don't wanna hear all that shit! Just be naked when I get back," he said then headed for the door.

"Hmmp! Yeah you wait on it," Tiffany capped back as she watched Randy walk out the front door.

Randy stepped foot out the front door and stopped in mid-stride. *"Holy shit,"* he said to himself, knowing that he had just fucked up.

Wolf and Ivy stood in front of Randy's house. Behind them stood forty Spades members all dressed in black with no nonsense looks plastered on their faces. In Wolf's hand, he held a shotgun.

"Where can I find Pauleena?" Wolf asked walking up to Randy.

"I..I..I don't know," Randy stuttered nervously.

"Get back inside the house!" Ivy barked pointing a 9mm at his head. "Now!" She grabbed Randy by the collar of his shirt and roughly forced him back inside the house.

"Fuck you doing back already I thought you were..." Tiffany's words got caught in her throat when she saw a man dressed in all black holding a shotgun walk through the front door followed by a woman dressed in all black holding a gun to Randy's head.

Tiffany quickly threw her hands up in surrender. "Listen I don't have nothing to do with him. I don't even like him," she began rambling. "As a matter of fact..."

KABOOM!

Randy watched in horror as the shotgun slug exploded in Tiffany's chest and sent her skidding across the living room floor.

"Please don't kill me man," Randy begged sounding like a bitch. Wolf trained his smoking shotgun at Randy's chest.

"Where can I find Pauleena?" Wolf asked dramatically jacking another round into the chamber.

"I swear to God I don't know," Randy pleaded.

"You better tell me something," Wolf pressed. He wasn't playing any games. He had a list of names and he planned on going down the list one by one until someone cracked and told him where he could find Pauleena. Until then anyone affiliated with Pauleena had to die and there were no exceptions.

"Nobody gets to speak to Pauleena. Shit I've never even seen her in person," Randy admitted. "Whoever this

Pauleena chick is, she's real organized. No one gets to speak to or see her. Everything goes through Prince and Prince deals with her directly."

"Then where can I find Prince?" Wolf asked. His patience was running thin, real thin.

"Please," Randy pleaded. "They'll kill me and my whole family. Here take the money and let me go and I promise you'll never see or hear from me again," he proposed. "Please I can't..."

POW!

Ivy put a bullet in Randy's head and watched his lifeless body crumble down to the floor. She stepped over the body as if nothing ever happened and grabbed the duffle bag from the floor as her and Wolf made their exit.

****

Wolf sat behind the wheel of the used minivan that he had purchased as him and Ivy rode in silence. Ever since their daughter Sunshine was murdered neither one of them were the same. It was like a piece of them had also died in that microwave. "You alright?" Wolf asked glancing over at Ivy for a second.

"I'm okay," Ivy replied placing a fake smile on her face. The truth was, she wasn't okay. She was forced to watch and listen to her daughter fry in a microwave. That image alone would forever play over and over again in her head. Pauleena had ruined her entire life. First she murdered Ivy's daughter and now she had Ivy in the streets murdering people like a common criminal. Ivy knew that what she was doing was wrong, but she convinced herself that she was doing it for her daughter, convinced herself that killing Pauleena was not only a must, but a need.

"What you over there thinking about?"

"Sunshine," Ivy replied quickly.

"How many times do I have to tell you that I'm sorry," Wolf said empathetically.

"Stop saying you're sorry!" Ivy snapped. "What happened to *"my"* daughter is not your fault and I don't want to talk about it no more!" Ever since Sunshine's murder, it seemed like Ivy was always in a bad mood and anytime Wolf tried to bring up their daughter she quickly shut his attempt down.

"Yes baby," Wolf said not wanting to cause an argument between him and Ivy. Ever since Sunshine was murdered Wolf noticed that Ivy had begun being mean and cold hearted towards him as if she blamed him or his past for getting their daughter killed. Wolf wanted to press the issue, but decided that now wasn't the time. He pulled the minivan into a parking spot at the hotel that the two were residing at.

Wolf and Ivy boarded the elevator and rode up to their floor in silence. When they entered their room, Ivy dropped the duffle bag down in the middle of the floor and headed straight for the bathroom. Second, later the sound of the shower being cut on could be heard. While Ivy showered, Wolf entered the bathroom, closed the lid, and then sat on the toilet.

"I promise we're going to find Pauleena and you'll have the opportunity to return the favor," Wolf told her. "But baby you have to keep a cool head and we have to be there for one another," he continued. "It seems like lately we've been drifting further and further apart from one another and I don't like it."

Ivy stepped out of the shower and grabbed a towel from off the wall unit and started to dry off. Wolf looked up into her eyes and saw that she was crying.

"Baby what's wrong?" he asked as he embraced Ivy in a tight hug. He could only imagine what was going on in her mind. Losing a family member or someone close to you was all-new to Ivy and all Wolf wanted to do was be there to comfort his woman when she needed him the most.

"I just need to be held," Ivy sobbed as she broke their embrace, walked out of the bathroom, flipped the covers back on the bed, and slid her nakedness in between the sheets. Wolf laid down behind Ivy in a spoon position and held her tightly as she cried her heart out for the remainder of the night.

"Everything is going to be okay baby," Wolf said as he tenderly stroked Ivy's hair until she finally cried herself to sleep.

CHAPTER 2

"Where's My Money"

"I'mma fuck this nigga Randy up," Prince said from the passenger seat as he puffed on a blunt. Randy was supposed to contact him and drop that money off to him three days ago. Prince called himself giving the man a seventy-two hour grace period to fix whatever it was that he had messed up, but now he had a change of heart and planned on killing Randy on site. "He know better than to play with Pauleena's bread."

"He gone learn today," Bobby Dread said from the back seat. Prince's job was to take care of all the business in the streets, while Bobby Dread's job was to protect and make sure that nothing happened to Prince. With so much heat coming down on Pauleena, she decided to go under the radar for a little while and let Prince handle things on the streets.

The driver pulled up in front of Randy's house and Prince and Bobby Dread hopped out of the vehicle followed by two young shooters who were dying to make a name for themselves. When Prince reached the front door, he immediately knew something was wrong when he saw that the front door was left cracked open. He quickly pulled his

9mm from his waistband and eased his way through the front door.

"Aw shit!" Prince huffed as he covered his nose and looked down at Randy and Tiffany's dead body. "Somebody clipped him and his girl."

Bobby Dread walked throughout the house looking around. In the past month, several members of their crew had been popping up dead and he planned on getting to the bottom of this situation. "Something ain't right," he said. "Our people have been dropping like flies. I want more muscle in all of our stash spots from now on," he ordered.

"You think that's necessary?" Prince asked taking the situation lightly. In his mind he didn't think anyone would be dumb enough to go up against them.

"That's your problem! You don't take things serious enough," Bobby Dread said. "Beef up the security until we find out what's going on." He wasn't about to take this situation lightly.

****

Later on that night, Bobby Dread hooked up with one of his best soldiers, a man that went by the name Big Tree. Big Tree stood around 6'7 and weighed about 260 pounds. He wore long rough looking dreads that looked like they hadn't been done or re-twisted since he started growing them. He also had a face full of rough looking facial hair to match. Big Tree took pride in hurting people and dishing out pain. He was a loyal man and would do anything for his mentor Bobby Dread.

Big Tree sat behind the wheel of the old Ford Explorer while Al Greene's "Love and Happiness" hummed softly through the speakers. Some nights him and Bobby Dread just rode around the city chopping it up with one another. Bobby Dread loved to ask his young protégé questions just to pick his brain. "What's your thought on all these random killings that's been taking place?" Bobby Dread asked staring blankly out the window.

"I think some fishy shit is going down," Big Tree said honestly. "It seems as if someone is targeting all of Pauleena's people."

"Yeah, but Pauleena has got so many enemies it's hard to pin point who might want her dead," Bobby Dread said.

"True," Big Tree agreed. "I was talking to some chick that's always in the middle of shit and she was telling me that she'd heard that Wolf and The Spades were back in town."

"Bullshit!" Bobby Dread said quickly. "We ran Wolf out of the city," he said still staring out the window. "He'd be a fool to come back on that trying to clean the streets up bullshit."

"Yeah that trying to clean up the world bullshit gonna fuck around and get his head blown off," Big Tree agreed. He wasn't around when Pauleena and her crew went head up with The Spades, but him along with the entire world had heard about it. Big Tree pulled up in front of one of Bobby Dread's homes and killed the engine.

Bobby Dread hopped out the truck when he spotted three figures dressed in black creeping from behind a van. Immediately Bobby Dread pulled his trench coat back brandishing his trademark A.K. 47. The quiet street quickly lit up with noise when the A.K. barked.

RAT, TAT, TAT, TAT, TAT, TAT!!!

The first three men that ran up were quickly put back down immediately. Bobby Dread spotted movement coming from his right. He quickly spun and opened fire. The A.K. rattled in his hand each time he let it rip. Bobby Dread heard the sound of a .45 being blasted behind him which told him that Big Tree had joined the gun fight.

Big Tree spotted two men dressed in black trying to creep up on Bobby Dread from behind. He quickly jumped in front of the three bullets that were intended for his mentor. Three bullets exploded in his bullet proof vest. The impact from the shots staggered Big Tree, but he was still standing. Big Tree fired round after round, but for each gunman he shot, it seemed like four more appeared out of nowhere. Before Big Tree knew it, he was out of ammo. "I'm out!" he yelled as several bullets tore through his upper and lower body.

Bobby Dread dropped as many of the gunmen as he could until a bullet pierced through his hand causing him to drop his A.K. Bobby Dread then quickly turned and tried to take off running. He'd only made it a few steps before several bullets tore through his lower body dropping him where he stood.

Big Tree on the other hand stood over Bobby Dread calling himself protecting his mentor. "Fuck you and your bullets!" he yelled as several bullets ripped and tore through his chest protector.

Once Wolf saw that the situation was under control, he quickly hopped out the van followed by three of his top lieutenants. He walked up to Big Tree who was doing his best to remain on his feet and put a bullet in his head; immediately dropping the big 6'7 monster. Wolf quickly looked down at Bobby Dread and remembered how deadly he was with his hands and ordered one of his lieutenants to hand cuff him. He sat back and watched as several Spade members roughly tossed Bobby Dread in the back of the van and peeled off just as quickly as they came.

CHAPTER 3

"Foolishness"

"Nah let me get the magnums," Live Wire said to the man that stood behind the counter of the bodega. He held up the line going back and forth with the man behind the register. Outside in the car Live Wire had some new young chocolate joint waiting for him. Tonight was her lucky night because not only was she able to hang out with Live Wire, but he was also going to allow her to suck his dick and in Live Wire's mind that in itself was a treat.

"Come on B. Knock it off," the man behind the register said and handed Live Wire a box of lifestyles condoms. "Take these. You know you can't fuck with them magnums," he joked laughing at his own joke.

"You a funny nigga," Live Wire said then tossed the box of condoms back at the man. He was kind of in a rush. After leaving the bodega Live Wire planned on heading to the liquor store and then straight to his shorty's crib. Just as he was about to pay for his condoms, Live Wire heard a deep voice boom from the back of the line.

"Damn nigga! What the fuck!" a big bald head man barked from the end of the line. "Fuck is you doing; buying the whole store or something?"

Live Wire turned and looked at the baldhead man like he had just lost his mind. "Fuck you just said?"

"No, no, no, not in the store. Take that shit outside," the man behind the register pleaded while praying that Live Wire would let the comments slide from the man at the end of the line. His prayers went unanswered when he saw Live Wire strike.

Before the bald head man knew what was going on, Live Wire had already hit him with a three piece that sent him crashing into the potato chip rack. Live Wire raised his foot and stomped the bald head man's face into the floor knocking out two of his front teeth. "Fuck outta here!" Live Wire growled as he tapped the bald head man's pockets and took all the cash the man had on him and then exited the store as if nothing had ever happened. Sitting in the passenger seat of his Benz sat Live Wire's new shorty, Nikki. Nikki was a young chick with a good head on her shoulders. Unlike Sparkle, Nikki was classy and carried herself like a lady at all times. In the looks department Nikki was average favoring the tennis star Serena Williams, but her body was flawless. She had the type of body that the average chick would pay for in a second. Unlike Sparkle, Nikki tried to convince Live Wire that he was better than a street dude. She stressed the value of education and told Live Wire that he could be doing so much more with his life.

Live Wire hopped back in the car still hype from the altercation that had just taken place in the store. "My bad baby... I just had to put hands on some clown in the store."

Nikki shook her head. "You have to learn to control your temper," she said placing her hand on Live Wire's thigh.

"Whatever you were in there fighting over, I'm sure it wasn't worth fighting over."

Live Wire thought about explaining how the bald head man had disrespected him, but quickly decided against it because he knew no matter how he explained it to Nikki, she still wouldn't understand. It was as if the two of them were born in two totally different worlds. In her mind she didn't believe that somebody talking shit was worth getting into a physical altercation over. She always stressed how words were just that, words, but not Live Wire. He was taught and raised that if anyone disrespected you, you had to do something to make sure that it wouldn't happen again.

"You wanna grab a bite before we head to the crib?"

"No I was going to cook for you," Nikki said smiling. "Naked in those new heels that you brought for me, but we can grab some take out if you want."

Live Wire smirked. "Home cooking it is."

Live Wire had copped a nice five-bedroom house for him and Nikki out in the suburbs. Nikki had just graduated from college and was just starting her career as a doctor. Live Wire planned on using Nikki to help him clean up his money and get certain things in her name that he couldn't get in his own name. He pulled in the driveway and killed the engine. When Live Wire and Nikki got out of the car, he saw a Range Rover swerve recklessly and then come to a halt at the beginning of their driveway. Live Wire already had his gun out and was about to clap something until he saw Sparkle hop out of the Range Rover flanked by her home girl Cindy.

"So this what you out here doing while I'm sitting in the house waiting for you to come home!" Sparkle yelled. Immediately Live Wire noticed neighbors porch lights come on followed by movement coming from their blinds and curtains. "Then you got the nerve to be cheating on me with this ugly ass bitch!" Sparkle barked as she tried to swing on Nikki, but Live Wire quickly stepped in front of her before she could connect. "Get off me, Live!" Sparkle screamed as she struggled to break free from Live Wire's grasp. While Live Wire held Sparkle back, Cindy crept around the other side of the car and stole on Nikki from behind. The surprise of the punch dropped Nikki and once she hit the ground, Cindy was all over her.

"Yeah that's right; fuck that bitch up!" Sparkle yelled looking on. Live Wire quickly snatched Cindy up off of Nikki and restrained her. As soon as Sparkle saw the opportunity, she took it. She quickly ran over and got a few good kicks in to Nikki's rib cage before Live Wire got her up off of Nikki.

"Chill the fuck out!" Live Wire yelled looking at Sparkle and Cindy as he watched Nikki hurry into the house.

"Told you this nigga wasn't shit!" Cindy spat looking at Live Wire with a disgusted look on her face.

Live Wire shot Cindy a look that said, *"bitch you better go get in the car before I slap the shit out of you."*

"I got this," Sparkle said to Cindy and watched as she took the hint and went and got back in the Range Rover.

"Fuck is you doing here?"

"No I should be asking you that!" Sparkle said snaking her neck. "You out here fucking these microwaveable bitches and then on top of that the bitches you out here fucking got the nerve to be ugly!"

"What you talking about that's just my *friend*," Live Wire lied.

"Oh my God! That bitch is so ugly!" Sparkle stressed. She knew the only thing she had over Nikki was her looks so she used the only ammunition she had. "Damn nigga you that desperate for some pussy that you out here fucking these Dracula looking ass bitches!"

"Yo chill!"

"Chill my motherfucking ass!" Sparkle snapped. "You bringing your ass home now!" she said grabbing Live Wire by the wrist and pulling him towards the Range Rover.

"Get off me!" Live Wire snatched his arm out of Sparkle's grip. He was just about to smack the shit out of Sparkle when he saw a police car pull up. Live Wire quickly stashed his hammer in the glove compartment of his car and locked the door before the cop got out of his car.

"Is there a problem over here?" The officer asked with his hand already on his holster.

"No it ain't no problem over here. We were just..."

"Sir I wasn't talking to you!" the officer growled cutting Live Wire off. He then turned his attention to Sparkle. "Are you okay ma'am?"

"Yes I am fine," Sparkle said wiping the tears from her eyes.

"Did this man put his hands on you?" the officer asked. "You can tell me. Ain't nothing going to happen to you while I'm here," he said confidently.

"Everything is good over here officer. We were just talking," Live Wire said.

"Sir I'm not going to tell you again to be quiet!" the officer warned.

"Fuck outta here nigga I can talk!" Live Wire spat waving the cop off. "I know my rights!" He then turned his attention back to Sparkle. "Now like I was saying baby..."

Before Live Wire could finish his sentence the cop pulled out a can of Mace and sprayed Live Wire's eyes. Once the cop saw Live Wire grab at his eyes, he quickly tackled him down to the ground. While the cop struggled to get the handcuffs on Live Wire, Sparkle crept up on the cop from behind and landed four quick punches to the back of his head as she tried to get the cop up off of her man. Minutes later, several police cars surrounded Nikki's house as Live Wire and Sparkle were arrested and taken to jail.

CHAPTER 4

"Where's Pauleena"

Bobby Dread looked around once the black pillow case was removed from his head. From the looks of it he was in someone's basement surrounded by a bunch of rough face looking men dressed in all black. Bobby Dread cleared his throat and spat on the floor. "Let's get this shit over with already!" he yelled showing no fear.

Minutes later, Wolf walked down the basement steps with Ivy fresh on his heels. The Spades weren't a gang and they weren't supposed to be out hunting people down. Their purpose was to clean up the streets, but once Pauleena murdered little Sunshine that changed everything. Now The Spades main objective was to kill Pauleena and anyone affiliated to her.

"Where's Pauleena?" Wolf asked standing directly in front of Bobby Dread.

Bobby Dread looked up at Wolf and smiled. "No speak no English!" There was no way he was going to give up Pauleena.

Wolf looked down at Bobby Dread and returned his smile. "Thought you might say something like that," he said then stepped to the side.

Ivy quickly stepped up. In her hand she held a thick chain that one would chain up a bicycle with. "Listen Dread," she began. "Pauleena killed my baby. I don't have no beef with you. All I want to know is where she is and I give you my word that I will let you go if you tell me where I can find her."

Bobby Dread looked up at Ivy and said, "No speak no English" and then busted out laughing as if he had just said the funniest joke in the world. Before Bobby Dread knew what had happened, Ivy had slapped him across the face with the chain. The rest of The Spade members looked on with a shocked expression on their faces as they watched Ivy beat Bobby Dread with the chain like a runaway slave.

"You...don't...speak...no...English…Huh? Well...me…either…motherfucker!" Ivy huffed as she swung the chain like a mad woman. The chain cut through the air making a whipping noise before sounding off loudly each time it connected. Ivy heaved heavily as she beat Bobby Dread with the chain for seven minutes straight until Wolf finally stepped in and grabbed the end of the chain before Ivy could swing it again. "Baby he's already dead," he whispered as he gently removed the bloody chain from Ivy's hand.

Ivy looked up at Wolf with specs of blood covering her face and smiled. "All he had to do was tell me where I could find Pauleena," she said with a crazed look on her face.

"I know baby," Wolf said in a calm tone as he placed a friendly hand around her shoulder and escorted her back upstairs. Ever since the death of little Sunshine he'd noticed that Ivy had been acting and moving like an entirely new person; a person he didn't recognize. One of Wolf's lieutenants, a man that went by the name Young Sam quickly ran up the stairs and caught up with Wolf before him and Ivy exited the premises.

"What you want me to do with his body?" Young Sam asked.

"Put it in a public place so all of his friends and family can see it and know that we are not fucking around and make sure you let them know that The Spades were responsible for his death," Wolf said as him and Ivy made their exit.

Once in the car, Wolf turned and looked at Ivy and decided to break the silence. "You alright?"

"Yes I'm fine," Ivy replied as if everything was normal. "I'm hungry. Lets go get some Popeye's."

"Why don't you cook tonight," Wolf suggested.

"Nah I don't really feel like it tonight," Ivy replied.

"You used to love to cook," Wolf said keeping his eyes locked on the road.

"Fuck is that supposed to mean?" Ivy asked defensively.

"Listen," Wolf began. He was tired of beating around the bush with her. "Ever since what happened to little Sunshine, you haven't been yourself! You don't do none of the things that you used to love to do or the things that made you, you!"

Ivy said nothing. She just stared blankly out the window. "All I'm saying is that I want my old Ivy back," Wolf pleaded.

"Yeah and all I want is my Sunshine back," Ivy countered slyly. She wasn't in the mood to hear what Wolf had to say tonight. In her eyes it would be stupid for him to expect her to stay the same with the mission at hand. In order to go after Pauleena, Ivy knew she would have to become just as heartless and cold blooded as Pauleena if she planned on taking her head on.

"Listen, I understand you are still going through losing Sunshine, but all this extra lip and attitude ain't doing shit but making things worse," Wolf told her. "I'm sure you can deal with this and still be respectful," he said as he parked in the Popeye's parking lot.

Ivy gave Wolf a sad look and then shook her head with a disgusted look on her face. "You sure have gotten soft," she said and then slipped out the passenger seat.

Wolf hopped out the Explorer and was over on the passenger side in about three steps. He grabbed Ivy and roughly forced her back until her back crashed into the passenger door.

Boom!

"Watch your mouth!" Wolf growled through clenched teeth with a finger pointed in Ivy's face. "I've been trying to be as reasonable with you as possible, but I swear you are working on my patience! This is the last time I'm going to tell you! Watch your mouth!"

"And what you going to do if I don't?" Ivy challenged. In her mind she felt that Wolf wasn't being as aggressive as he should have been or riding as hard as he should of been riding for his daughter and that's what disturbed her the most. "I'm out here riding for mines and you got a problem with that!?"

"That's not my problem," Wolf replied. "You have to learn when to turn this off baby. You can't be like this 24/7. When I was out in the streets I was one way and every night when I came home, I was a totally different person. You know why?" he asked, but didn't give Ivy the opportunity to answer. "Because I know how to turn that shit off and on."

Tears poured from Ivy's eyes. "I'm sorry Wolf, but this isn't me. I'm supposed to be raising my baby right now not out killing and murdering like some common criminal and once it's cut on I don't know how to turn it off. You are going to have to help me," she cried. "I already lost my baby. I can't lose you as well," she cried even harder. Wolf could tell that she was fighting with the demons that were deep down inside of her. When an innocent person is forced to kill, there is no telling how the ending will turn out.

Wolf was just about to pull Ivy in for a hug when he heard loud footsteps approaching followed by a deep voice boom from behind him.

"Ma'am you alright over here?" a big dirty looking white truck driver asked with his partner bringing up the rear.

"Yeah we fine. Me and my girl was just talking," Wolf said politely.

"I don't reckon I was talking to you boy!" the truck driver snapped making sure he dragged out the word boy. He then turned his attention to Ivy. "Ma'am is this man causing you trouble?"

"No we're fine; thank you," Ivy told the truck driver.

"You sure?" the truck driver asked Ivy, but was staring at Wolf like he wanted to do something.

"Yo my man," Wolf began. "Tonight is not the night. Please go on about your business." He was two seconds off the white man's ass and he didn't even know it.

The truck driver took an aggressive step forward with his fist balled up. "I'm about sick and tired of your mouth boy!"

Wolf sighed loudly as he turned and stole on the truck driver. The punch echoed loudly throughout the parking lot. The truck driver shook the punch off and put his head down and rushed Wolf back into the hood of the Explorer where the two traded blows. Just as Wolf began to get the best of the truck driver, his partner snuck up on Wolf from behind and threw him in a choke hold.

"Go to sleep!" the truck driver's partner growled as he applied more pressure to the choke hold.

Once Ivy saw Wolf steal on the truck driver, she was getting ready to jump in the fight and hold her man down when she saw the truck driver's partner throw Wolf in a choke hold and try to squeeze the life out of him. Ivy quickly removed a knife from her pocket and pulled the blade out with a snap.

"Motherfucker!" Ivy growled as she plunged the knife in and out of the white man's neck repeatedly. "Didn't I tell you stupid ass crackers to leave us the fuck alone?!"

Wolf sucked in as much air as he could when he felt the big white man's arms loosen up from around his neck. He was just about to breathe a sigh of relief when he felt something warm and wet splash down onto his face. *"What the fuck?"* he said to himself when he touched his face and his fingers came away bloody. Wolf looked behind him and saw Ivy standing behind him with a bloody knife in her hand. Before he could say anything, Ivy had moved onto the original truck driver. Wolf watched as Ivy stabbed the white man repeatedly. From the look in her eyes, Wolf could tell that she was enjoying the horrible act she was committing. Wolf stood there and looked on for a few more seconds before he grabbed Ivy and pulled her up off the truck driver. Ivy struggled to break free from Wolf's grasp. "Baby he's dead," he whispered in her ear and escorted her back to the truck. Wolf quickly hopped behind the wheel and pulled off before any new customers pulled up. He glanced over at Ivy and noticed that she still had a crazed look in her eyes. Things were beginning to go too far and Wolf was afraid that Ivy would lose herself in between the madness.

"You alright?"

Ivy nodded her head and then continued to stare blankly out the window.

Wolf pulled into the parking lot, killed the engine, and quickly hopped out the truck and walked around to the passenger side. He opened the door, pulled a red handkerchief from his back pocket, wet it with his tongue, and cleaned the specs of blood from Ivy's face. "Let me see your hands."

Ivy held her hands out and they too were covered in blood. Wolf grabbed the bottle of water from the console and wet Ivy's hands with some water. He did his best to clean them with the handkerchief.

When the two made it upstairs to their room, Ivy stripped down naked and hopped in the shower. Wolf sat on the edge of the bed and just stared at the wall. He knew Ivy was just trying to help, but he was afraid that the death of Sunshine had her going crazy. Ivy wasn't thinking rational and she was making decisions off of emotion without thinking things through first. Wolf knew if she continued to move like that, she would get herself killed sooner than later and that was something that he couldn't allow.

Wolf heard the shower cut off and two minutes later Ivy stepped out the bathroom butt naked. She kissed Wolf on the cheek, pulled the sheets back, and hopped in the bed. "Good night."

Wolf paused for a brief second and then said, "good night baby."

CHAPTER 5

"You Mad"

L ive Wire sat in the booth of an expensive restaurant. Across from him sat Sparkle. She was dressed in a nice silver dress, but anyone that knew her could tell that she wasn't happy.

"You haven't touched your food baby. What's wrong?" Live Wire asked as if he didn't know what the problem was. It had been two days since him and Sparkle had been released from the precinct.

"Don't really have an appetite right now," Sparkle said taking a deep sip of her glass of wine.

Live Wire shook his head. "Nothing ever makes you happy."

"How you expect me to be happy when you out here fucking random ugly ass bitches," Sparkle said sucking her teeth. "You playing yourself!"

"You still on that?" Live Wire huffed. "Shit happened over a week ago. Let that shit go already," he said as his iPhone buzzed notifying him that he had just received a text message. Live Wire read the text, replied, and closed his phone. When he looked up, Sparkle was looking dead at him.

"Well?"

"Well what?" Live Wire countered.

"Who was that texting you?"

"None of your fucking business," Live Wire said looking at Sparkle like she was crazy. He loved Sparkle to death, but he was starting not to like her anymore. She was turning into a jealous nag and she didn't even realize how close to getting kicked out of the whip she was.

"Probably that ugly ass bitch you were with the other night," Sparkle spat with venom in her voice. "Whack ass bitch!"

Live Wire gave Sparkle a sad look. "All you chicks believe that if a woman doesn't *look* better than you, then she can't be an upgrade," he chuckled. "If you believe that, then you're dumber than you look."

Sparkle tried to come up with a good come back line, but she couldn't think of one so she tossed her drink in Live Wire's face and stormed out of the restaurant leaving Live Wire sitting in the restaurant alone.

Live Wire sat at the table for five minutes before he headed outside hoping to find Sparkle. When he stepped foot outside the restaurant, he looked up and down the street and saw that Sparkle was long gone. "Fuck!" Live Wire cursed. He knew he may have went a little too far back in the restaurant. Instead of meeting Sparkle at the house, Live Wire decided to give Sparkle a little space. He hopped in his Benz and headed uptown to holler at his right hand man, Bills.

****

Bills stood leaned up against his Range Rover listening to one of his workers explain why he hadn't yet finished the last package that was laid on him. The worker's story sounded genuine, but Bills still wasn't sure if the man's word could be trusted or not. "You know what's going to happen if I find out some funny shit going on; right?"

"Come on Bills. How you gone insult me like that? I've been getting money with you and Live Wire for years. I would never violate like that," the worker said.

Bills saw Live Wire's Benz pull up across the street and decided to dismiss the worker in fear that Live Wire would turn the situation into something that it didn't needed to be. "Yo listen, just finish that package and report back to me in twenty-four hours," he said dismissing the worker with a warning.

"How we looking out here?" Live Wire asked as he gave Bills dap.

"Walk with me," Bills said as the two men started down the block. "We might have a situation that may need some looking into."

"What's up?"

"Just hollered at one of our workers," Bills began. "He was telling me that shit done slowed up because some new jack nigga calls himself opening up in the projects a few blocks away from one of our spots."

"This nigga with Pauleena or something?" Live Wire asked. To stop all the beef, Live Wire and Prince had both agreed that Pauleena would take one part of the city as her territory and Live Wire would take the other. Each one knew not to violate the other. Pauleena ran her side and Live Wire ran his side and everyone was happy, but now a new nigga wanted to open up shop and it had to be in Live Wire's territory.

"Nah he out here by himself," Bills told him.

"Word?" Live Wire said scratching his chin. "What's this niggas handle? I may have heard of him."

"The nigga name is Avon. That's all I know," Bills said.

"You know where he be at?" Live Wire asked.

"You already know." With that being said, the two men hopped in Bills Range Rover and headed downtown towards the projects.

CHAPTER 6

"Can't We All Just Get Along?"

Avon sat sunk down in the passenger seat of the Yukon staring blankly out the window. On his lap rested a fully loaded .45. He wasn't the one to do a lot of talking. His motto was actions would always speak louder than words. For all his life Avon had been selling drugs. He started out in Baltimore, and then expanded out to Texas, and now his next stop was New York. Avon had gotten word that the entire city of New York's drug trade was being ran by a woman; some chick named Pauleena. After giving the idea a lot of thought, Avon had decided that he wanted in on some of her real estate. Not being the type to try and negotiate, Avon decided that he was just going to open up shop and let the chips land where they may. He'd deal with the drama later. Right now his main focus was getting this money.

Behind the wheel of the Yukon was Avon's main shooter, Smokey and in the back seat was his back up shooter, a chick that went by the name Kyra. Kyra was a slim chick with a nasty attitude. She wore baggy jeans, a t-shirt, and on her head she wore her hair cornrowed going to the back with a black Brooklyn Nets fitted on top of her braids. In her waistband rested a .357 that she couldn't wait to shoot. "What's the plan if this Pauleena chick act like she want problems?" Smokey asked.

"We don't deal with problems," Avon said with a smirk. "We cause the problems."

Smokey pulled up in front of the projects and double parked. Seconds later a worker named Tyrone walked up to the window and stuck his head in the passenger window. "What's goodie?" He asked giving Avon dap.

"Everything straight?"

"You already know," Tyrone boasted. "Got shit jumping like the playoffs out here."

"The playoffs, huh?" Avon asked looking at the clown that stood before him. "Listen, I'mma have Kyra swing by tomorrow and hit you with another package. Make sure you have that bread ready for me, a'ight."

"You already know I got you bro. I'm out here all day and all..." The Yukon had already pulled off before Tyrone could even finish his sentence. "Bitch ass niggas!" Tyrone spat once the Yukon was down the block. Two minutes after the Yukon had pulled off, Tyrone noticed a Range Rover pull up. Two men hopped out the Range Rover and headed straight for Tyrone.

****

Live Wire walked up and stopped directly in front of Tyrone. "I'm looking for Avon. Where can I find him?"

Tyrone looked from Live Wire to Bills. "I don't know no Avon," he said and tried to spin off, but before he could even take two steps, Live Wire smacked him in the back of his head with a 9mm.

"Get the fuck over here!" Live Wire growled as he snatched Tyrone up by the back of his collar and slammed him back up against the black gate. "Listen, you make sure you tell Avon that he's got forty-eight hours to remove his peoples from my territory. Oh yeah and by the way, the name is Live Wire." Live Wire cocked the 9mm back and a bullet popped out the chamber and into his hand. He then turned and tossed the bullet to Tyrone. "Tell Avon the next one gone have his name on it!" he said as him and Bills walked off leaving Tyrone standing there with a silly look on his face.

Back in the Range Rover, Bills and Live Wire rode in silence. Live Wire still couldn't believe that someone had the nerve to try and open up shop in one of his territories.

"You good?" Bills asked pulling up next to Live Wire's Benz.

"Yeah I'm good," Live Wire lied. "I'mma scream at you tomorrow," he said and then exited the Range Rover.

Live Wire cruised through the city in deep thought. Things had been going good for him business wise. The last thing he needed right now was to have to kill some loser over a couple of dollars, but that was the game. Not wanting to go home and have to deal with Sparkle's bullshit, Live Wire decided to go to Nikki's house instead. At least there he knew he would be welcomed with open arms and not have to deal with any foolishness.

Live Wire pulled into Nikki's driveway and killed the engine. He walked up to the front door, stuck his key in the door, and entered the house. Inside he found Nikki sitting on the couch with a glass of wine next to her and a mystery novel in her hand.

"Heeeeey baby!" Nikki said excitedly as she hopped up off the couch and ran into Live Wire's arms. She wrapped her arms around his neck as he effortlessly lifted her up. Nikki quickly locked her legs around Live Wire's waist and planted wet kisses all over his face. All she had on was a matching orange bra and thong set and her hair was tied up in a scarf.

"I missed you so much," Nikki whispered in Live Wire's ear as she ran her tongue across his earlobe. Live Wire carried Nikki over to the counter and sat her on top.

"Oh look what I found," Live Wire said as he slid the front of Nikki's thong to the side. There was a furnace between her legs. Live Wire ran his fingers across her clit. Nikki jerked and tightened her thighs around his hand. Then she caught her breath and relaxed. Live Wire grabbed Nikki's ankles as he ran his tongue down her toned calves until he made his way down to her toes. He sucked her toes and slid a finger inside of her at the same time. The act seemed to drive Nikki wild as she began to gyrate her hips further into Live Wire's hand. "Please come fuck me," she begged. "Fuck me!"

"Shut up!" Live Wire growled as he snatched Nikki's thong off and tossed it over his shoulders. "Pull them titties out!" he demanded as he lowered his head in between her legs.

"Oh my fucking God!" Nikki yelled as she felt Live Wire's mouth make contact with her swollen clit. The loud slurping sounds that escaped from in between Nikki's legs only turned her on even more. Live Wire lifted his head back and spit on Nikki's pussy, then nastily slurped it all back up. This was an act that caused Nikki's orgasm to erupt in a series of waves.

Live Wire then roughly snatched Nikki off the counter and spun her around forcing her to bend over and grip the counter. Nikki was getting ready to protest when she felt Live Wire's tongue slide down the crack of her ass.

"Mmmm...." Live Wire moaned as he ate Nikki's ass like it was puppy chow. His tongue worked over time as he lapped at her walls with his tongue. Once Live Wire was done, Nikki was breathing like she had just ran a marathon.

"Oh you thought I was finished?" Live Wire said with a smirk as he held his dick in his hand stroking it gingerly.

"No please! I can't take no more," Nikki submitted. Live Wire ignored Nikki's weak plea and tossed her back up on the counter on her side.

Nikki was on her side with her right leg in the air and her limbs loose. Live Wire moved in and out of her. Her body was lean and more flexible than it had appeared. Nikki craned her head back for a kiss. She sucked Live Wire's tongue like she hadn't been fed sensuality in a long time.

"Yes...yes...yes!" Nikki moaned with each stroke that was delivered. Live Wire fucked her, fucked her harder, fucked her like he had just been released on a ten year bid from prison.

"Arggggh!" Live Wire groaned as he pulled out and painted Nikki's ass with his white seeds.

"Why didn't you let me suck it out?" Nikki whined with a disappointed look on her face as she looked back at the semen on her ass.

"Next time baby," Live Wire said out of breath as he flopped down on the couch.

"I know that look," Nikki said as got up and joined Live Wire on the couch. "Wanna talk about it?"

"Gotta push some clown's wig back," Live Wire shrugged.

"For what?"

"Clown calls himself opening up on my territory."

"So you are going to kill another black man, because he's trying to make money just like you?" Nikki asked. "You want to kill him, but aren't you out doing the same exact thing?"

"That's not the point," Live Wire snapped.

"Then what is the point?" Nikki capped back. She didn't understand why a black man would kill the next black man just to make a point.

"We come from two different worlds so you wouldn't understand," Live Wire said waving Nikki off. She was always trying to preach that black power shit and right now Live Wire wasn't in the mood to hear that shit.

Nikki placed her hand on Live Wire's thigh. "You don't even know your own worth. If you could put together one of the biggest movements since the Black Panthers, imagine what you could do if you went to college and got a degree. In six years you'd be running a Fortune 500 company," she pointed out. "All I'm saying is, you're better than this street bullshit and you know how this story ends."

"Stop acting like you care about a nigga," Live Wire joked. He knew everything that Nikki was saying was true, but this was his life or better yet the life that chose him.

"Promise me you won't kill that brother," Nikki said looking in Live Wire's eyes.

Live Wire pulled Nikki in close for a hug. "No promises baby," he said and left it at that.

CHAPTER 7

"This Big Show"

Y ou ain't saying shit nigga!" The Big Show growled. He stood on the basketball court shirtless trying to guard a slim kid named Ben that was supposed to be the next big basketball superstar. Ben was a good kid that didn't really hang out very much. He was mostly home taking care of his little brother or either in the gym working on his game. Ben usually didn't play random pickup games, but on this particular day he was walking home from the store when he was challenged by The Big Show to a game of one on one. Ben tried to refuse, but it seemed like the more he refused, the more aggressive The Big Show and his crew became so he decided that one game wouldn't hurt; or would it? The score was 12 to 0 and the game was to 21.

Ben skillfully dribbled the ball through his legs toying with The Big Show. He caught him with a series of street moves and then finished him off with a fade away jumper that was all nets. Onlookers oohed and ahhed every time Ben crossed The Big Show up.

"14 to zip," Ben said with a smirk on his face as he dribbled the ball through his legs never taking his eyes off of The Big Show. "Quit now while you ahead."

"Shut the fuck up and play ball!" The Big Show snarled as he got serious. He was now determined to steal the ball from Ben and keep him from scoring.

Ben faked left, faked right, then threw the ball through The Big Show's legs and zipped by him. Ben went up for the lay up when The Big Show jumped up and tackled him in mid-air.

"Get that weak shit outta here nigga!" The Big Show barked as if what he had done was perfectly legal. The truth was Ben was making him look like a fool on the court and the fact that he couldn't beat the young man pissed him off.

"Foul nigga!" Ben yelled as he shot back to his feet.

"Stop crying lil nigga," The Big Show said as he forcefully threw the ball at Ben's face, but his reflexes were on point so he caught it. "Play ball!"

Ben dribbled the ball through his legs again. The hard foul had pissed him off. Now he was determined to do The Big Show in. He hit The Big Show with a series of moves causing all of the onlookers in the park to go crazy and cheer. The Big Show's sneakers squeaked loudly as he tried to keep up with the quickness of Ben, but the young man's skills were just too much for him. Ben hit The Big Show with a mean cross over and tried to zip passed him, but The Big Show stuck out his arm and clothes lined Ben down to the ground like he was rag doll. Ben hit the ground hard holding his throat. The Big Show stood over Ben and was about to taunt him when he heard a strong voice from behind him yell.

"Fuck is you doing!" a man wearing a du-rag barked from the sideline. "Take your ass whipping like a man!"

"Fuck is you talking bout?" The Big Show spat inches away from the man's foot. "The lil nigga went up and I challenged him and I'mma challenge him every motherfucking time! You got a problem with that?"

The man with the du-rag didn't want any trouble, but he had known Ben since he was a kid and didn't want The Big Show and his crew to take out their anger on him or maybe even do something that would cause the young man his career. He decided to step up to the plate and take one for the team. He figured that way; Ben could live to see another day. Ben had a promising future while the man in the du-rag had wasted most of his life in and out of prison. The man in the du-rag gave Ben a private look, took a deep breath, and then spoke. "Nigga suck my dick!" As soon as the words left his lips, a bottle was shattered over his head followed by several fists that came from all angels. The Big Show and his crew stomped the man in the du-rag out until he was no longer recognizable. Ben looked on in horror before finally picking himself up off the ground and hauling ass out of the park.

"Talk that shit now!" The Big growled as he watched his troops demolish the man with the du-rag. Ever since The Big Show had taken over what was left of The Spades, you couldn't tell him anything. He walked, talked, and acted as if the streets were his. The beeping of a car horn grabbed The Big Show's attention. He looked up and saw Prince hop out of an all-white Range Rover flanked by two shooters.

"That's enough!" The Big Show barked to his troops as he headed over towards the Range Rover."What's good my nigga?" He greeted Prince with a hand shake followed by a hug.

Prince glanced over in the park and then back at The Big Show. "Everything good?"

The Big Show shrugged. "Yeah you know. I had to teach a nigga some manners."

"We got problems," Prince said with his voice turning serious. "Grab a few of your men and follow me," he said as he hopped back in his Range Rover.

The Big Show snatched up four of his best shooters, hopped in his Audi and followed Prince's Range Rover. After a thirty-minute drive, The Big Show followed the Range Rover in an alley in the back of a restaurant. From a telephone pole, The Big Show could see a man's body hanging. He quickly hopped out of the Audi, looked up, and saw that the body that was hanging from the phone lines belonged to Bobby Dread. "Who's responsible for this?"

"You can't read?" Prince asked nodding towards Bobby Dread's naked body. Across his chest someone had carved "The Spades," more than likely with a knife.

"The Spades?" The Big Show echoed with a confused look on his face.

"You didn't have anything to do with this; did you?" Prince asked in an accusing tone.

"What are you asking me?" The Big Show asked. "I would never violate like this and you know it."

"Well if you didn't do it, then that only leaves one person...Wolf!" Prince said staring up at Bobby Dread's lifeless body.

"You think Wolf is back in town?"

Prince shrugged. "I don't know, but lately a lot of our men have been coming up missing or either dead and besides," he paused for a second. "Who else you know that would have been able to do this to Bobby Dread?"

"You right," The Big Show agreed. "This is what we going to do. Put the word out that we're willing to pay a lot of money for the whereabouts of Wolf or anyone associated with him."

"A'ight and stay on point and get someone to cut down Bobby Dread's body," Prince said as he opened the door to his Range Rover.

"And where are you going?" The Big Show asked.

"I'm going to tell Pauleena about our little problem," Prince said and then pulled out of the alley disappearing around the corner.

CHAPTER 8

"Quality Time"

Ivy sat on the bed in the hotel room cleaning her 9mm with a dirty rag. In her spare time the diva used to like to get her nails and feet done, but now it seemed like all she cared about was killing or doing harm to someone. Ivy sat on the bed in a daze and wondered how she'd feel and react when she finally came face to face with her daughter's murderer. Ivy looked down at the gun her hand and for the first time she realized that she was no longer the loving woman that she used to be. She was now a monster on a path of destruction. She couldn't even remember the last time her and Wolf had sex or the last time she'd even said anything nice to him for that matter. It was as if all she thought about all day was killing Pauleena. Ivy tossed the 9mm on the bed and buried her face into her hands. *"You better get it together or else you going to lose a good man; a real good man,"* she said to herself. Ivy loved Wolf to death, but she was obsessed with killing Pauleena.

The sound of Wolf entering the hotel room snapped Ivy out of her thoughts.

"Hey baby," Wolf sang with a smile on his face. "You hungry?"

"Kind of."

"Good. Get dressed," Wolf said as he tossed two bags on the bed.

Ivy grabbed the bag and pulled out a gorgeous black dress. "It's beautiful," she said holding the dress up against her body.

"I'm taking you out tonight," Wolf told her. "We're going to go out and have a good time just like the good old days."

"What about finding Pauleena?"

"Fuck Pauleena! We'll find her another day," Wolf said. "But tonight is all about us."

Ivy nodded her head. "You know I love you right?"

"I know baby," Wolf replied. He knew Ivy needed a break. She needed something that would take her mind off of Pauleena for a day, something that could spark the fire back into their relationship. The restaurant he planned on taking Ivy to was just the breath of fresh air that Ivy needed.

Ten minutes later Ivy stepped out of the bathroom looking like a completely different woman. "How do I look?" She smiled and stood in the doorway striking a pose.

"Good enough to eat," Wolf said honestly as he checked out the beauty that stood before him. He aggressively pulled Ivy in close for a hug, leaned over, and whispered in her ear. "I'm going to gobble you up when we get back," he said through clenched teeth.

"You promise?"

"I can show you better than I can tell you," Wolf countered as he smacked Ivy on the ass as she walked by.

****

Once Wolf got behind the wheel of the car, he felt Ivy lean over and plant a series of soft kisses on his neck while her hands unfastened his belt. Wolf couldn't remember the last time he and Ivy had been intimate with one another and to be honest he was loving every second of what was going on. "That's right, pull that dick out," Wolf coached as he watched Ivy handle her business. Once Ivy finally got a hold of Wolf's dick, she put it in her mouth and sucked on it real slow. She moaned from deep within like it was the best thing she had tasted in a while. Ivy slid her hand up and down Wolf's shaft as she tried to suck the life out of him. Her other hand cradled his balls as she reminded him who his one and only was.

Wolf threw his head back and let out a soft groan. He ran his fingers through Ivy's hair and enjoyed her mouth. Greedy sounds escaped from Ivy's lips as her head began to bob up and down faster and faster. Wolf held on to the back of Ivy's head because he was trying to hold out for as long as he could, but Ivy was giving him no choice. Her mouth was furious, wet, and loud.

Ivy's moans got louder and louder as she began to suck harder and even faster. Wolf looked around and noticed that the windows were now fogged up. He looked over and Ivy now had her ass hiked up in the air while she went to work on him. Wolf firmly grabbed the back of Ivy's head and released his fluids.

"Arrrgh!" Wolf roared as he shot his load. He thought he was about to lose his mind when Ivy continued to suck after he was already done. "I can't take no more. You got it," Wolf submitted.

"You tapping out?" Ivy looked up with a wicked smirk on her face.

"Yes baby I'm done."

"Say I'm the woman."

"You the woman baby! You the woman!" Wolf said out of breath.

"That's what I thought. Now let's get to this restaurant because I'm starving."

****

The food in the restaurant was amazing. Both Wolf and Ivy destroyed their food, but instead of eating dessert the two decided to order two bottles of wine, relax, and enjoy each other's company.

"I miss this," Ivy said lifting her glass to her mouth.

"What? The wine?"

"No not the wine silly," Ivy laughed. "I miss this meaning me and you having a good time together."

"I miss this too," Wolf said. His hand found its way under the table and somehow on Ivy's thick thigh.

"I'm telling you now, you get this pussy wet and you going to have to fuck me all night," Ivy said in a sexually charged voice.

"Is that right?"

"Yup," Ivy said licking her lips. The wine had her even hornier than ever. She wanted to pull out Wolf's dick right there in the middle of the restaurant and ride it in front of everybody, but she knew that would have to wait until they returned back to their room. Ivy hadn't realized just how long it had been since the last time Wolf took care of her pussy. "Keep talking because the more you talk, the worse you making it for yourself," she warned him.

"Am I supposed to be scared," Wolf chuckled as he took another sip from his wine. Wolf was getting ready to say some freak shit when he noticed Ivy's whole mood change.

"What's wrong?" he asked as he noticed Ivy staring blankly over his shoulder. "Baby you alright?"

"Pauleena," Ivy whispered.

"What about her?"

"She's sitting right there at the table behind you," Ivy said with fire dancing in her eyes. She immediately grabbed her purse and pulled out her .380. "I'm going to take her right here in the restaurant."

"You can't," Wolf said. "We'll take her when she goes outside. It's too many witnesses in here."

"Fuck that! We might not ever get another chance like this again," Ivy said as she discreetly slipped her heels off of her feet under the table. "It's either now or never," Ivy said as she got up from the table.

"Fuck!" Wolf cursed as he pulled his .45 from his waistband and followed Ivy's lead.

CHAPTER 9

"Let's Get This Party Started"

Pauleena sat at the table sipping on a glass of wine. To her right was her right hand man and head of her security, Big Ock. In total Pauleena was surrounded by five of her finest Muslim bodyguards. She had so many enemies that she had to be on point at all times. Sitting across from Pauleena was a Columbian man that went by the name Alvarez. Alvarez was a good friend of Pauleena's connect, a man that went by the name Chico and it was safe to say that Chico wasn't happy with the way that Pauleena had been handling her business so he sent Alvarez to go have a talk with her.

"You understand what I'm saying?" Alvarez asked.

"Yeah I hear you," Pauleena said dryly. She had just received a text informing her that Bobby Dread was found dead hanging from a light pole and she wasn't really in the mood to hear or entertain what Alvarez was saying at the moment.

"All of the shoot outs and killings are going to have to stop. It's bad for business," Alvarez said. "And honestly Chico is fed up with all of the bad coverage you've been getting on the news."

"Listen Alvarez," Pauleena said in a slur. "I understand what y'all are saying, but y'all make it sound like I like getting into shoot outs and damn near getting my head blown off. I'm doing the best I can out here and please take into consideration that I am a woman and I'm out here all by myself," she pointed out.

"Not our problem,"Alvarez said simply. "The more you're in the paper or involved in shoot outs, the more likely you are to give somebody up from our camp if you're ever faced with some serious numbers and that we can't and won't allow to happen."

"I don't know who the fuck you think you're talking to, but you better act like you know," Pauleena spat. "I've done two prison bids!" she said holding up two fingers for extra emphasis. "And I ain't never told on anybody or dragged anybody down with me. I've been a stand up woman since I came in this shit and that's how I'm going to leave!"

"Why are getting so upset? Did I push a wrong button?" Alvarez grinned. "Listen all I'm saying is this, you need to tone it down out here or risk getting cut off or worst."

"What do you mean by worst?"

"Worst means you being killed," Alvarez said honestly. "Chico sent me here to talk to you because he likes you, but enough is enough. We run a smooth operation, a quiet operation, and let's be honest, if we were to ever cut you off we'll probably have you killed shortly afterwards because the big bosses can't risk you talking because you're bitter about being cut off. All I'm asking is that you tone it down out here. Chico really likes you and wants to continue to do business with you, but you are going to have to tone it down, no ifs, ands, or buts about it."

Pauleena thought about saying some slick shit, but decided to hold her tongue. "Listen Alvarez please tell Chico that I appreciate him for even giving me the opportunity to get money on this level and I'll do my best to tone it down out here. The last thing I want is him as an enemy," she said humbling herself.

"I'm sure he'll be glad to hear that," Alvarez smiled.

Pauleena got ready to say something else, but paused when she saw Alvarez's head get blown off right in front of her. Pauleena looked up into the eyes of Alvarez's killer, a woman in a nice black dress. Pauleena couldn't pin point where she'd seen the woman before, but her face did look familiar. Pauleena went to reach for her gun when Big Ock quickly tackled her out of her chair down to the floor as the sound of several different guns could be heard being fired. From there all hell broke loose.

Wolf shot one of Pauleena's bodyguards in the face as he pushed Ivy out of the line of fire and took cover behind a booth as bullets flew from all directions. Wolf knew that him and Ivy would be out gunned, but now it was too late to turn back. On a silent count of three, Wolf sprung from behind the booth and fired three quick shots that connected with his intended targets Then he ducked back behind the booth.

"Come on get up," Big Ock said as he lifted Pauleena up to her feet. He got ready to escort her out the back door when he noticed that she was bleeding. "You hit?"

"I'm good!" Pauleena said as she pulled out a 9mm and returned fire as Big Ock rushed her through the kitchen. Before Pauleena made it through the double doors she looked back and spotted Wolf and the woman in the black dress chasing behind them.

"Oh shit!" Pauleena yelled as she fell. The tall heels she wore weren't made for running.

"Come on!" Big Ock yelled as he dragged Pauleena across the dirty kitchen floor by her arm. He knew that he was hurting her arm, but at the moment his main objective was to keep Pauleena alive by any means necessary and that's just what he was going to do.

Pauleena quickly kicked off her heels and scrambled back up to her feet as several bullets whizzed by her head. She ran through the kitchen and fired four reckless shots over her shoulder not caring who she hit.

Big Ock and Pauleena made it out of the kitchen and found themselves running down a small hallway. Pauleena was running when out of nowhere she was roughly tackled down to the floor. When she turned over she saw that it was Wolf who had tackled her. Before she could do anything, Wolf blasted her in the face with two vicious punches that would knock most men out, but not Pauleena. She tucked her chin and took the blows well. Before Wolf could follow up, Big Ock rewarded him with a swift kick to the face.

Pauleena quickly scrambled to her feet as she heard Wolf and Big Ock getting busy in the middle of the hallway. From how loud and noisy the fight was, Pauleena knew that, that fight would be a fight to the death. She wanted to help Big Ock, but she knew at the moment that wasn't an option. Right now the only thing on Pauleena's mind was getting away. She made it a couple of steps when she felt someone grab a handful of her hair. Pauleena spun around and found herself looking down the barrel of a big hand gun.

Ivy pressed the 9mm into Pauleena's forehead and pulled the trigger.

CLICK

CLICK!

When Pauleena realized that the gun was empty she quickly grabbed Ivy's head with both hands and rammed it into the wall. She followed up with a knee to the pit of Ivy's stomach. Pauleena didn't know who the chick in the black dress was, but she had no problem beating her ass. "Bitch!" she barked as she landed two loud punches to Ivy's face.

Ivy tried to swing, but Pauleena held her at bay by her hair. The grip that she held on Ivy's hair limited her movement. Not having any other option, Ivy grabbed Pauleena's nipple and gave it a hard twist.

"Arhhhhg!" Pauleena squealed as she released Ivy's hair. Before she got a chance to regroup, Ivy landed a straight right hand that snapped Pauleena's head back and had her nose bleeding profusely. The site of her own blood lit a fire inside Pauleena. She responded with a quick right hook that landed on Ivy's temple. The blow stunned and staggered Ivy, but she somehow kept her footing. Before Pauleena could land another punch, Ivy ran full speed and hit Pauleena hard and forced her back. The two went crashing forcefully through the staircase door and down the top flight of stairs. Pauleena and Ivy went violently tumbling down the stairs until the metal landing broke their fall.

"Fuck," Pauleena mumbled as she slowly pulled herself up to her feet. She looked over and saw that Ivy was lying flat on her back unconscious. Pauleena took a close look at the woman in the black dress and then it all started to come back to her. Pauleena remembered the woman in the black dress crying and begging her not to put her baby in the microwave. She looked down at Ivy and smiled. "Silly ass bitch!" Pauleena huffed as she raised her foot and stomped Ivy's face into the metal floor before taking off down the stairs. Pauleena wanted to kill Ivy right then and there, but that was a task that she would have to save for another day.

Right now Pauleena's main focus was getting away freely. As she ran down the stairs, she clutched her shoulder that was bleeding. Pauleena exited the staircase and found herself in some underground parking lot. She stopped and looked at her reflection in a car mirror and frowned. Her face was a bloody mess. Pauleena took her elbow and shattered the driver side window of a random parked car. Once inside the vehicle she tried to hotwire the car, but had no luck.

"Shit!" Pauleena cursed as she exited the parking lot and just as luck would have it, there was a cab sitting on the corner looking for a passenger to pick up. Pauleena quickly dived in the back seat of the cab and shouted out an address. She made sure she kept her head ducked low as several police cruisers passed by the cab. Once Pauleena was out of harm's way, she breathed a sigh of relief. "I'm going to kill Wolf and his bitch!"

****

Big Ock's head snapped from side to side with each blow that Wolf landed. After realizing that he was no match for Wolf's hand skills, Big Ock began to back pedal away from the fight in an attempt to escape. Wolf looked down and picked Big Ock's gun up from off the floor. He aimed and pulled the trigger. Wolf watched as Big Ock grabbed his stomach and doubled over in pain before dropping down to one knee.

"Please... Please...," Big Ock pleaded with a scared look in his eyes. "Please don't kill me."

Wolf ignored the Muslim's cry, pointed the gun at Big Ock's face, and pulled the trigger.

CLICK!

CLICK!

A smile crept on Big Ock's face when he realized that the gun was empty. "You bitch ass nigga," he said gaining his confidence back. "You lucky I...."

Wolf stood over the big man in the suit and slapped him across the face with the gun.

WHACK! "You talking all that shit!"

WHACK!

"What I told y'all niggas about playing with me!?"

WHACK!

"I'm a bitch ass nigga!?"

WHACK!

"You had something to do with killing my daughter!?"

WHACK!

"Huh!?"

WHACK!

WHACK!

WHACK!

WHACK!

Wolf went to swing the gun again when he felt someone grab his arm from behind. He spun around and saw Ivy standing there.

"We have to go Wolf," Ivy said in a gentle tone. She looked down and could no longer recognize the big man in the suit. Wolf had beat the man to a pulp.

"Where's Pauleena!?" Wolf barked breathing heavily.

"She got away," Ivy replied with a defeated look on her face. "But we have to go," she said as she rushed Wolf down the stairs out into the underground parking lot.

"Hold on!" Wolf said as he noticed the parked car with the window busted out. He quickly slid behind the wheel, leaned over, and unlocked the door so Ivy could get in. Wolf then pulled out a pocketknife and worked his magic. Two minutes later, he pulled out of the parking lot. Wolf and Ivy made sure they looked straight ahead, as they rode right pass the police like nothing ever happened.

"You alright?" Wolf asked as he glanced over and noticed that Ivy had some dried up blood around her nose along with a bruise under her eye.

"I'm good," Ivy said as she stared blankly out the window.

"We'll get her the next time," Wolf said trying to lighten up the mood.

"I let her get away," Ivy said in a voice just above a whisper. "What if there's no next time? I fucked up!"

"It's okay baby," Wolf said placing a calming hand on Ivy's thigh. He knew it was going to take Ivy a while to get over letting Pauleena slip through her fingers. "Thank you for coming out with me tonight. You looked very nice."

"Thank you," Ivy smiled as tears ran down her face.

"We gonna be alright baby. I promise," Wolf said. For the rest of the ride back to the hotel neither one said another word to the other.

CHAPTER 10

"I Don't Care"

Steven sat in the bed reading a new book he had just downloaded on his kindle. Laying with her back turned to him was his wife Ann.

"Baby I'm sorry, but what was I supposed to do?" Steven asked.

"It was our anniversary for Christ sakes!" Ann snapped.

"I'm a doctor Ann. What was I supposed to do; not answer my pager? It was an emergency," Steven said. "What can I do to make it up to you?"

Before Ann could respond, the couple heard someone ringing their doorbell repeatedly. Steven glanced over at the digital clock that rested on the nightstand that read 1:34 am. Steven had a scared look on his face as he slid out of the bed. Whoever had been ringing the doorbell was now banging on the door forcefully as well. "Stay right here," Steven told Ann as he headed downstairs to see who was banging on his door at this time of night.

"Who is it?" Steven called out.

"Open the motherfucking door!" the voice on the other side of the door yelled.

Steven opened the door and Pauleena spilled in through the front door dripping blood all over the place. "What the fuck!?" she barked. "I was ringing the doorbell for an hour!" Pauleena exaggerated. She walked over to the kitchen table and knocked everything onto the floor with a swipe of her arm. She then climbed up on the table and laid down. "Doc I need you to fix me up!" she said as she removed her shoulder holster, blouse, and then bra.

"Is everything alright down there?" Ann asked as she started down the stairs and saw a topless woman lying across her kitchen table leaking blood all over the place.

"Everything is fine baby," Steven said quickly. "I need you to run upstairs and grab my work bag and bring it down stairs," he said as he watched his wife trot back up the stairs. Steven grabbed a clean towel from the linen closet and pressed it against Pauleena's wounded shoulder. "Keep pressure on it," he told her as Ann returned back downstairs with his bag. "Thanks baby."

Pauleena winced in pain as Steven worked on her shoulder. "I'm sorry for just showing up at your door step Doc."

"Don't worry about it," Steven said. He was pissed that Pauleena had come to his home spilling blood everywhere, but he knew the payday was going to be huge. "You know you going to have to slow down out there in them streets, right?"

"Yeah I know Doc," Pauleena said in an uninterested tone. After nearly getting her head blown off, Pauleena wasn't really in the mood for someone to be preaching to her.

Forty-five minutes later, Pauleena was all stitched up.

"You're the best," Pauleena said placing a kiss on Steven's cheek. "I'll have someone drop some cash off to you tomorrow."

"No problem," Steven replied. "Just next time please try not to come to my home. I try to keep my personal and business life separate, you know?"

Pauleena smiled. "I'll have someone get in touch with you tomorrow," she said and then left. Outside an all black Expedition sat waiting curbside for her arrival. A big Muslim bodyguard hopped out the passenger seat and held the back door open for Pauleena.

As soon as Pauleena hit the back seat, the Expedition immediately pulled out into traffic. In the back seat sat Prince with a concerned look on his face. "You good?"

"Yeah I'm good," Pauleena said accepting the drink that Prince handed her. "I'm going to kill that motherfucker Wolf!"

"I knew he was back!" Prince snapped. "A lot of our men have been getting hit and coming up missing and I couldn't figure out who was behind it."

"Yeah, Wolf and his bitch tried to take me out," Pauleena fumed. Her mind quickly went back to the day when she stuck Ivy and Wolf's baby in the microwave. She knew that by not killing Ivy that day it might come back to haunt her. "I need you to find out where Wolf and his bitch are hiding for me. I got something special for them."

Pauleena was getting ready to say something else when the driver suddenly stomped down on the brakes bringing the Expedition to a screeching halt. Before Pauleena knew what was going on, two minivans surrounded the Expedition.

"What the fuck?" Prince yelled as he removed his 9mm from his waist. He then quickly handed Pauleena his back up .380. A Mexican looking man quickly snatched open the back door and out of reflex Pauleena shot him in the face. She turned to shoot the next man, but quickly had a change of heart when an A.K. 47 was pointed in her face.

"Drop your weapon now!" the Mexican looking man barked in broken English as he roughly snatched Pauleena out of the truck where several Mexican looking men stood holding machine guns.

"What's this all about?" Pauleena asked with her hands up in surrender.

"Chico wants to see you!" the man holding the A.K. said as he roughly tossed Pauleena in the back of one of the vans and pulled off.

All Prince could do was sit there and watch as the gunmen took Pauleena away. He prayed that Pauleena would made it back alive.

CHAPTER 11

"Shots Fired"

Avon sat on the passenger side of the Yukon as he listened to his worker give him the run down on the latest events. "So you said his name was Live Wire?" he asked.

"Yeah him and his man rolled up on me like they was ready to get busy," the worker told him. "Talking about you was in his territory."

"So what was he trying to say? I can't eat?" Avon asked.

"Basically…"

Avon turned and looked at Smokey. "You ever heard of a Live Wire?"

"Yeah he supposed to be some hot head that used to be down with The Spades back in the day," Smokey answered. "He's known for letting them thangs fly."

Avon smiled. "Good. I want you and Kyra to find out where this clown be hanging out at and let him know that we let them thangs fly too."

"I don't know if that's a good idea," the worker said with a nervous look on his face. Unlike Avon and his crew, the worker had lived in New York all of his life and had saw firsthand how Live Wire and The Real Spades rolled. He knew how they got down and he knew the consequences that came behind fucking with a man like Live Wire. "Live Wire's crew is deep out here in these streets."

"Nigga you sound scared!" Kyra snapped as the back door to the Yukon opened and she stepped out.

"Nah I'm not scared. I'm just saying that Live Wire and his crew...."

"What? You one of Live Wire's hoes or something?" Kyra spat. Before the worker could reply, Kyra's hand moved in a blur as she sliced the side of the workers face with the razor she held in her hand.

The worker wanted to rip Kyra's head off but he knew if he laid a finger on her that he would leave with more than a scar on his face, so instead he just stood there looking stupid holding the side of his face while blood ran through his fingers.

"Bitch ass nigga!" Kyra barked as she cleared her throat and spat in the workers already bloody face and then she hopped back in the Yukon.

"Listen," Avon said getting everyone in the truck's attention. "I'mma need you two to spread the word that we not fucking around out here in these streets. If Live Wire wanna play, then we gonna play."

"The not fucking around crew," Smokey said smiling as he pulled off.

****

Live Wire laid naked flat on his stomach on the king sized water bed with his eyes closed while Nikki straddled his lower back giving him a much needed strong handed massage. For the past week, Live Wire had been spending more time with Nikki and he had to admit he was really beginning to fall in love with her. Nikki was different from the type of women that Live Wire usually dealt with and the fact that it was something new turned Live Wire on even more. The other day Nikki had taken Live Wire to his very first stage play. At first, he was against it, but when the show was over he had to admit it wasn't as bad as he thought it would be.

"What do you want to do tonight baby?" Nikki asked planting a big wet kiss on Live Wire's lips.

"I don't wanna do shit but taste this pussy all night," he said with a devilish grin on his face.

"She can't take no more," Nikki laughed as she hopped up off of Live Wire and walked over to the entertainment system and turned on some slow jams. "How about I make my man a nice home cooked meal?"

"What you trying to do; get me to love you even more?" Live Wire sat up on the bed. He was about to pull Nikki down on the bed and have his way with her mouth until the sound of his iPhone ringing grabbed his attention. Live Wire reached over and grabbed his phone off the night stand. He glanced down and saw Bills name flashing across the screen.

"Yo what up?" he answered.

"We got a problem," Bills said. "Meet me at the spot."

"Say no more." Live Wire ended the call and quickly began getting dress.

"Is it that bad?" Nikki asked as she watched Live Wire get dressed in a hurry.

"Yeah," Live Wire answered as he kissed Nikki on the forehead. "I promise I won't be back too late."

"I know you have to handle your business. Just promise me that you'll be careful," Nikki said with her voice full of concern. "I'll still cook and just put your food in the microwave for you just in case you get home late, you can still eat."

Live Wire was used to having to argue when he had to break off plans with women. Nikki was really becoming a breath of fresh air and he was thankful to have a woman like her in his life. "Thanks baby. I'll call you when I get a chance." He kissed Nikki on the lips and quickly rushed out the door.

Live Wire hopped in his Benz and pulled out into the streets like a mad man. Bills couldn't tell him exactly what was going on over the phone, but from the tone of Bills voice, Live Wire could tell that whatever happened was a serious matter. Live Wire doubled parked the Benz in front of a bodega that Bills and a few of his main shooters stood in front of.

"What's good?" Live Wire said giving Bills and the rest of the shooters dap.

"We got a problem," Bills began. "Remember that new cat, Avon?"

"Yeah what about him?"

"Him and a few of his shooters rolled through and shot up one of our spots," Bills explained. "Two of our guys were shot, but nobody got killed."

The more Live Wire listened, the angrier he was becoming. There was always a young punk who felt that the world owed him something and dying to be made an example out of. "We have any info on this clown, Avon?"

"Some cat from Baltimore who supposed to hold a little weight," Bills answered.

"I want to know everything about this fuck nigga by tomorrow morning." Right then and there, Live Wire knew he would have to make an example out of the young hustler.

"No there's more," Bills said. "Wolf is back."

"Fuck outta here," Live Wire said in a disbelieving tone. "I thought he retired?!"

"I heard Pauleena killed Wolf's daughter," Bills began. "Put the little baby in the microwave," he said shaking his head in disgust.

"You serious?" Live Wire said in shock. He hadn't spoken to Wolf in a few years, but that was still his brother.

"Yup," Bills nodded. "I heard Wolf and Ivy ran down on Pauleena at some restaurant and aired the whole shit out."

"Find out where I can find Wolf. He might need our help," Live Wire said as he felt his phone buzz on his hip. He looked down at his phone and saw he had a text message from Sparkle.

SPARKLE: If you think, I'm going to let you and ya new bitch just ride off into the sunset you're sadly mistaking!

SPARKLE: After all the shit, I done been through with you oh you must got me fucked up!

SPARKLE: ??????

LIVE WIRE: leave me alone thx..

SPARKLE: I swear to god I'm going to kill you and that ugly ass bitch!

SPARKLE: I hate u!

LIVE WIRE: enjoy the rest of your night 😎

SPARKLE: oh u think I'm playing? Watch this MF!

Live Wire put his phone away. He didn't have time to play with Sparkle. At the moment he had more important things to deal with. He turned to Bills and before he could say another word, he felt his phone buzz again. Live Wire looked down at his phone and saw that Sparkle had sent him a picture of all of his clothes and sneakers cut up. *"This bitch is crazy,"* he said to himself.

"Yo, find out what you can about that clown Avon and we'll go handle that tomorrow and if you get any information on Wolf's whereabouts hit my jack," Live Wire said as he gave Bills dap and hopped back in his Benz and pulled off. As Live Wire cruised the streets, he felt his phone buzz again. He looked down and saw he had another text message from Sparkle. It was a picture of a bed covered in money. Underneath the picture the text read.

SPARKLE: nigga you got 20 min to get here b4 I burn all this shit!

"Shit!" Live Wire cursed loudly. He knew he should have been removed his safe from the house, but he never imagined that Sparkle would take things this far. He stomped down on the gas pedal and gunned the engine as he headed to Sparkle's house.

CHAPTER 12
"Enough Is Enough"

S parkle paced back and forth in her master bedroom as she sipped on a glass of Coconut Ciroc and orange juice. To say she was mad or upset would be an understatement. She couldn't believe that Live Wire was really trying to leave her for some new fake booshie chick that had to nerve to be ugly. It had gotten so bad that Live Wire even refused to answer her calls and text messages. Sparkle knew the only way to get Live Wire to come and talk to her would be to threaten to burn his money. She had on a white wife-beater and a pair of black leggings with a scarf tied around her head. On the outside, Sparkle was mad, but on the inside, she was hurt at how easy it was for Live Wire to just kick her to the curb like she was some random chick he'd just met.

Just as Sparkle refilled her glass with more Ciroc, she heard a car pulling into the driveway. Before Live Wire had arrived, Sparkle was feeling brave and tough, but now that he was there, it was a whole different story.

Fabolous' new album hummed through the speakers at a low volume as Sparkle heard Live Wire's footsteps growing louder and louder.

Live Wire burst into the bedroom with a mean look on his face. "Fuck is your problem!?"

Sparkle went to respond, but her head snapped back from the backhand that was delivered to her face. Live Wire roughly grabbed Sparkle by her neck and forced her back into the wall.

"This what you want right!" he yelled. "You begging me to put my foot up your ass!" He raised his hand to strike her again.

Sparkle ducked and covered her face with her hands anticipating the blow that never came. "All I want you to do is love me!"

"So you think by cutting up all my shit gonna get me to love you!?" Live Wire yelled.

"I'm sorry!" Sparkle cried. "I need you Live Wire! Please don't leave me. I don't know what I would do without you," she admitted. Live Wire turned and looked down at the bed covered in money.

"You were gonna burn my money?"

"No daddy, I would never do that. I was just trying to get you to..."

Live Wire roughly tossed Sparkle down on the bed that was covered with money. "What I told you about playing with me!?" he growled as he pulled Sparkle's leggings down to her thighs and watched her big ass spill out. Before Sparkle could respond, Live Wire pulled out his already hard dick and jammed it inside of Sparkle from behind with force.

"Ahhh, ahhh I'm sorry daddy!" Sparkle yelled out in a mixture of pain and pleasure.

Live Wire roughly grabbed a handful of Sparkle's hair causing her head to jerk back as he tried to pulverize her insides.

Live Wire spanked Sparkle's right cheek and then the left cheek. He did that over and over again to let Sparkle know who was boss. He moved slow, kept control, and slowed down his pace a little not wanting his energy to spill too early. "Throw that ass back!" he demanded and immediately Sparkle obliged. She arched her back, spread her legs, and bounced her huge ass back and forth just the way she knew Live Wire liked it. Yeah Sparkle was mad with Live Wire but she couldn't deny the fact that she loved him more than anything in this world.

Live Wire watched as Sparkle's ass loudly slapped against his torso. He then grabbed Sparkle's hips firmly and went yet deeper. Sparkle's moans deepened as her nails dug into the pillow.

"Harder," she moaned. "Fuck me harder!"

Live Wire fucked her harder, fucked her like he was trying hurt her, fucked her like he hated her, fucked her like an animal.

Sparkle buried her face inside a pillow as she enjoyed the pleasure and pain she was receiving. Moans that started off soft now became desperate. Live Wire stayed behind her and dipped to get a better angle. His thrusting was deep, steady, and powerful.

"This my pussy?" Live Wire barked. "Huh!?

"Yes daddy!"

"I can't hear you!" he shouted as he slapped her ass with force.

"Yes daddy! This all your pussy!" Sparkle yelled. She loved every minute of the dick action Live Wire was giving her.

Live Wire delivered six more powerful strokes before pulling out and coming all over Sparkle's ass.

Once Live Wire was done, he laid back on the bed covered in bills and just stared up at the ceiling. At the moment his mind was all over the place. Not only did he not know what he was going to do about Sparkle and Nikki, but the news about Wolf's daughter being murdered wasn't sitting too well with him either. Not to mention he knew the streets would be looking for him to respond to Avon's latest attack. Live Wire's thoughts were interrupted when he felt Sparkle crawl onto the bed and lay her head on his chest.

"I'm sorry daddy," she whispered. "I promise I'll buy you some more clothes."

Live Wire didn't even respond, instead he continued to stare up at the ceiling until the two fell asleep on the bed covered in bills.

CHAPTER 13

"Surprise, Surprise"

The Big Show sat on a stool at the bar of a five star hotel. It was a little early in the day to be having a drink, but today just happened to be one of those days. The fact that Wolf and the few followers he had left were out to kill him and everyone associated with Pauleena added stress to his life. Not to mention Pauleena was now missing. He had gotten word from Prince that Pauleena had been abducted by some Colombians.

"You okay baby?"

Sitting next to The Big Show sat a thick light skin chick he met off of Instagram. After seeing a few half naked pictures of the woman, The Big Show just knew he had to sample some of her goods. "Yeah I'm good. I just got a lot on my mind," he said taking a sip from his drink.

"After we finish getting our drink on, I promise I'll make sure your mind is clear and the only thing you are focused on is me," light skin said in a seductive tone. It was the middle of the day, but she was dressed as if she was headed to a nightclub. She had on a short royal blue dress that just barely covered her ass with a pair of five inch royal blue pumps.

"Is that right?" The Big Show smirked as he downed the rest of his drink with one gulp. Light skin thought that she hit the jack pot when he hollered at her on Instagram, but little did she know that after she gave up that pussy, The Big Show had no plans of ever seeing her again.

"Yup," light skin smiled.

"I'll be right back. I'm going to the bathroom and then we can go upstairs to our room," The Big Show said as he got up and headed to the restroom. The Big Show entered the restroom and headed to the urinal. Just as he got ready to release himself, a white guy came and stood at the urinal right next to The Big Show.

"Damn!" The Big Show snapped. "It's at least four urinals open and you pick the one right next to me? Fuck is you; a faggot or something?"

"Hey man it's a free country and I can take a piss where I damn well please!" the white guy capped back matching The Big Show's attitude.

The Big Show's hand moved in a blur as he stole on the white guy. The right hook landed perfectly on the white guys chin and put him to sleep. The Big Show then stood over the white guy, pulled his penis out, and began to urinate all over the white guys face. Once The Big Show was done, he delivered a hard kick to the white guy's stomach before turning and exiting the restroom. Once outside the restroom, The Big Show headed back towards the bar where his new friend sat waiting patiently for him. After what had just happened in the restroom, The Big Show badly needed to unwind and relieve some stress. The Big Show suddenly stopped in mid-stride and froze. His eyes were locked on a familiar face, a face he thought he would never see again.

Standing over by the elevator stood Ivy. At first, The Big Show thought his eyes were playing tricks on him, but upon further review he was positive that the woman standing by the elevators was in fact Ivy. Thoughts of going over there and snatching Ivy up out of the hotel crossed his mind, but after giving the idea some thought, The Big Show quickly decided against it. There were way too many witnesses not to mention cameras in the hotel. Besides, The Big Show knew that if Ivy was in the hotel that Wolf couldn't be far behind. He quickly pulled out his cell phone and called Prince. On the fourth ring, he finally answered.

"I found Wolf and his girl Ivy. Round up all the shooters. It's time to end this chapter once and for all!"

CHAPTER 14

"Columbia"

Pauleena was escorted off the jet and rushed into an awaiting limousine. On the entire ride on the jet, Pauleena thought that she was being brought to Columbia to be murdered, but then it dawned on her that if the Columbians wanted her dead, then they damn sure didn't have to bring her all the way out to Columbia to make that happen. "Where are we going?"

"Shut up!" A short Columbian man with a mean scowl on his face capped. The limousine held five armed Columbian men all who looked like they would put a bullet in Pauleena's head at a seconds notice. At the moment, all Pauleena could do was sit back and just enjoy the ride. After about an hour drive, the limousine went from a smooth ride to a rough bumpy one. The nice road suddenly turned into a dirt road. Right then and there, Pauleena knew they would be arriving to their destination soon. The limousine drove along a palm tree lined road which led to an enormous Spanish mansion with the most spectacular garden Pauleena had ever seen. The limousine reached a metal gate where an armed guard quickly walked up and spoke briefly with the driver before they were allowed onto the property. The limousine cruised for about another four minutes before finally coming to a stop. Pauleena was then roughly snatched from the back of the limousine and escorted inside the mansion. Guarding the front door stood four armed soldiers ready to kill at the drop of a hat. Pauleena's bare feet walked across the marble floor until she reached the den where she was ordered to have a seat. Out in the hallway she could hear men speaking loudly in Spanish. Then minutes later, Chico entered the room and immediately all the chatter ceased.

Chico was a handsome Columbian man in his early forties. Just his presence alone spoke volumes. He wore an expensive platinum suit and in his hand he held a drink. "So finally we meet at last," Chico said with a smile as he walked over and kissed Pauleena on the cheek.

"Excuse my appearance, but I was told I had to come here on short notice." Pauleena looked down at her dirty feet and smiled. This was her first time meeting Chico in person. Over the years she'd only been allowed to deal with Alvarez.

"I'm just glad you could make it," Chico said helping himself to a seat right next to Pauleena. "I'm going to get straight to the point," he began. "You have been making too much noise over the past few years and my partners and I like to move in silence if you know what I mean?"

"I understand but..."

"What happen to Alvarez?" Chico asked cutting Pauleena off.

"He was just at the wrong place at the wrong time," Pauleena said. She knew the type of danger she was in and how violent the Columbians were known to be. She just hoped and prayed that everything ended up fine.

"Alvarez was a good friend of mines," Chico said taking a deep gulp from his drink. "What happened?"

"I ran into some old friends while Alvarez and I were having our meeting," Pauleena said nodding down to her shoulder that was positioned in a sling.

"Listen Pauleena, I'mma cut to the chase. Either you tone it down in the streets or we can no longer do business with you!" Chico spat. "And if we cut ties that means you die!" He paused for a second. "You know a lot and we can't risk you running your mouth."

"I would never snitch!" Pauleena snapped. "I've been selling drugs all my life and been to jail more than once and never once opened my mouth!"

"I understand. I'm just letting you know that if you don't tone it down, then the outcome won't be pretty," Chico said calmly.

"Well I don't know if you've noticed, but I'm a woman and in this business the last thing a man wants to hear is that a woman is in control, so I have to go above and beyond to prove myself and let people know that I belong! I'm sorry, but there's no way to do that quietly!" Pauleena said with much attitude.

"Not my problem," Chico said simply. "Either you turn the heat down or else the heat is going to be turned on you!" he told her. "My advice to you is to hire someone to run things for you and move back out to Miami and enjoy your money."

"All the money I bring in and you bring me here to threaten me?"

Chico chuckled. "This is not a threat! This is a warning! The higher ups already want you out, but I told them to give you one more chance."

"Thanks!" Pauleena said rolling her eyes. She couldn't believe that after all the work she had put in over the years, she was now being threatened. It was hard to keep a low profile when ignorant people only respected violence. While she was out in the trenches, Chico was in his mansion counting his money so she knew he'd never understand her point of view.

"Alvarez was a good friend of mines, but now he's dead because of you and I still spared your life," Chico said.

"I said thank you. What more do you want?" she asked with a stank attitude.

"Come with me to dinner," Chico said with a smile.

"Do I have a choice?"

"No!"

****

Later that night Pauleena found herself in an expensive restaurant and sitting across from her was Chico. It was obvious that in Columbia he was the man. Pauleena admired the way people treated Chico and how his presence demanded respect. He was a well-known billionaire, a drug God, and he had an army behind him that was willing to risk their lives to protect his. Chico was what Pauleena saw herself being in a few years; that was if she could stay alive.

Chico took a sip from his wine and smiled. "What?"

"Nothing was just admiring you."

"Me or the power that I have?" Chico asked with a raised brow.

"Both," Pauleena answered truthfully.

"You want to know something," Chico asked not giving Pauleena a chance to respond before he continued. "You can be bigger than this. All you have to do is stay focused and stop with all the killing and wild, wild, west antics. If you really want to do this the right way, I'll show you the way."

Pauleena smiled as she took a sip from her wine. "I hear what you're saying and you make it sound so easy."

"Life is only what you make it."

"Well maybe your life, but mines is a little more complicated," Pauleena confessed.

Chico reached under the table, grabbed Pauleena's leg, removed her shoe, and placed her foot on his lap as he gave her foot a nice slow massage. "You are a beautiful woman Pauleena and I respect your honesty, but more importantly I respect your loyalty," he said. "In my world a woman is not supposed to be on the front line risking her life let alone her freedom."

"Well..." Pauleena shrugged. "This is my life." She knew the way she lived was wrong, but she had to do what she had to do.

"You are already a millionaire no?" Chico asked.

"Yes I am," Pauleena answered proudly. Only she knew all the hard work it took her to be in the position that she was in. Not to mention that was something that no one could ever take away from her.

"I want you to come live with me," Chico said. "Come and live and be treated like the queen that you are."

"What exactly are you saying?"

"I'm asking you to be my lady," Chico stated plainly. "With me and you together, there won't be no stopping us."

"You barely even know me."

Chico chuckled. "I know more about you than you think," he said as he placed Pauleena's foot on his penis.

Pauleena's eyes widened with excitement when she felt Chico's manhood rise through his slacks. She then began to rub her foot up and down on her own. "Oh really, tell me what you claim to know about me."

"I know that you need a man like me," Chico told her. "I know with me as your partner, there's no telling the heights we could both reach and I also know that no other man will ever take better care of you than me," he said in a matter of fact tone. "I also know about your problems back home with Wolf and The Spades." His last comment hit Pauleena hard. "I could have Wolf and his whole crew killed like that!" Chico said snapping his fingers for extra emphasis. "At the rate you're going, you're either going to end up getting killed in the streets or either I'm going to be forced to send a hit squad to the states to kill you." Chico paused. "I'm trying to give you a way out Pauleena. Let me help you."

Pauleena thought about it for a second while Chico massaged her foot under the table. Everything that Chico said made perfect sense, but there were some things that she just had to do herself. "I hear what you saying Chico, but you don't understand. Wolf and The Spades killed my mother so I can't just leave it alone or just let someone else handle that for me." She looked Chico in the eyes. "I wasn't raised like that. I'm sorry, but I was raised to handle my business."

"And I respect that. I really do, but it's to the point that the higher ups are fed up with you and your shenanigans. I'm trying to help you, but soon there's not going to be much I can do to help you," Chico said honestly. He liked Pauleena and he stuck his neck out there for her many of times, but soon there would be nothing he could do to help her.

"Why do you want to help me so bad anyway?"

"Cause I see something in you that you don't even see in yourself," Chico said.

After dinner, Pauleena and Chico couldn't keep their hands off of one another in the limousine on their ride back to

Chico's mansion. The limousine pulled onto the estate and Chico and Pauleena slid from the luxury car hand in hand. As Chico and Pauleena approached the door of the mansion, one of his guards opened the door before he even reached it. He closed the door and the two just stood in front of each other in the foyer. "Before you leave I want you to really think about being my lady," Chico said as he easily removed the straps of Pauleena's dress from her shoulders and watched the dress fall to her feet. A smile quickly appeared on Chico's face when he saw that, Pauleena didn't have on any panties. She stood before him as naked as a newborn looking like a sexy work of art. Chico took a second to admire her beauty before he walked up to her and pressed his lips against hers and slipped his tongue in her mouth. Chico then took a step back and removed his clothes until he too stood butt naked in the foyer. He grabbed Pauleena's hand and led her through the mansion and into the kitchen where he grabbed a bottle of wine. Chico opened the bottle with a corkscrew and then led Pauleena out back to his outside Jacuzzi.

As Pauleena followed Chico out to the Jacuzzi area, she couldn't help but notice that Chico's bodyguards were trying their hardest not to take in all of her nakedness.

Chico entered the Jacuzzi first and watched as Pauleena slowly entered the water. He took a sip from the bottle of wine and then held it out towards Pauleena. She took the bottle and took a deep gulp.

"This is the life," Chico said smiling. "Just pick up and do whatever you want without having to worry about shit!"

"Can you see yourself loving a woman like me?" Pauleena asked. "I ain't going to lie; I'm known to be a handful," she said flashing a sly smirk.

Chico smiled and took a swig from the bottle of wine. "I love a challenge!"

"And I love a nice size dick," Pauleena whispered in Chico's ear as she dipped her hand in the water and began fondling Chico's package. This was the moment she'd been waiting for all night. It had been almost two years since the last time the sexual beast inside of Pauleena had been fed. Between her legs was a throbbing sensation and she couldn't take it anymore. Pauleena plucked the bottle of wine from, Chico's hand, took a swig, and then sat the bottle down on the edge of the Jacuzzi. "You wanna be my man?"

Chico nodded yes.

"We'll come fuck me like you want to be my man!" Pauleena demanded. Chico pulled Pauleena close and shoved his tongue in her mouth as their bodies met. He lifted Pauleena up and instantly her legs clamped around his waist. Their tongues did a slow dance as Chico slowly carried Pauleena out of the Jacuzzi and laid her down on her stomach on a nearby beach chair. Pauleena tried to turn around, but Chico slapped her ass with force letting her know that she needed to just stay put for now.

SLAP!

"Don't you dare move this ass without my permission!" Chico growled as he roughly grabbed a handful of Pauleena's hair yanking her head back forcing her to look at him. "Do I make myself clear!?"

"Oh yes daddy," Pauleena purred in a sexually charged tone. If it was one thing that Pauleena loved, it was a man that knew how to take control in the bedroom. Chico released Pauleena's hair and began planting soft kisses on her lower back. He worked his way down from her lower back to the crack of her ass where he let his tongue explore her back door.

"Ahhh yeah slurp that shit!" Pauleena growled through clenched teeth as she arched her back so Chico could really get in it.

Chico quickly made his way from Pauleena's ass down to her sopping wet pussy. She had already spread her legs open in hopes that he would taste her sweet wet pussy. "Mmmmmm!" He let out a loud moan as he licked, slurped, and sucked on Pauleena's swollen clit from behind. From the way Pauleena was moaning, he could tell that she was enjoying the feel of his tongue. Chico flicked his tongue like a lizard. Then he began moving his tongue in a slow circular motion forcing Pauleena to climax sooner than she had planned. Pauleena tried to get up, but, Chico held her down and continued to work his tongue like a rattle snake; both torturing and pleasing Pauleena at the same time. She felt like she was about to die when Chico slurped loudly on her swollen sensitive clit. Chico had such a firm grip on her that all Pauleena could do was sit there and take it like a big girl.

Without warning Chico flipped Pauleena over on her back and entered her walls slowly. The two looked in each other's eyes and shared a long drawn out kiss as Chico invaded her insides with his dick. He stroked her hard and fast. He did that until she came and when she came he still didn't stop. He kept going until Pauleena tried to push him away. The only problem was, Chico wasn't going away. He wasn't going to be pushed away. He held Pauleena like she was his prisoner. From her facial expressions and her loud moans he could tell that she loved everything he was doing. Pauleena grabbed Chico's ass and pulled him in deeper. Her breathing was just as thick and as hot as it was between her legs. "I love this dick," Pauleena moaned as she dug her fingernails down into his skin deep enough to leave a mark.

Chico readjusted himself and pinned Pauleena's legs back to her ears, gritted his teeth, and fucked Pauleena like his life depended on it. Instead of pulling out, Chico decided that it was too good so instead he let out a loud growl and erupted inside of Pauleena.

"I don't want you to leave me?" Chico whispered as he played in Pauleena's hair. He could definitely see himself being with a woman like her for a very long time. Besides Chico needed someone to keep him company in his large house.

"No promises but I'll see what I can do," Pauleena said and then kissed him on the lips.

"Pauleena I don't want nothing bad to happen to you."

"I'm a big girl," Pauleena smiled. "I'll be fine," she said with confidence.

"Please don't forget the spot light is on you," Chico pointed out. "Please promise me you'll tone it down out there in them streets. I don't want anything bad to happen to you."

"How about I make you a promise," Pauleena said as she curled up in Chico's lap.

"I'm listening."

"Give me two months to get back and clean up everything I need to clean up and I promise I'll be back, but this time it will be to stay," she smiled.

"That's your word?"

"That's my word baby," Pauleena smiled. "All I need is two months."

"Pauleena please listen to me carefully," Chico said with his voice turning dead serious. "Tone it down and handle whatever it is you have to handle...QUIETLY! There's a target on your back and I would like for you to make it back to me in one piece."

"Stop worrying so much baby," Pauleena said planting a wet kiss on Chico's lips. "Two months and I'll be back... I promise!"

CHAPTER 15

"What Now"

Wolf hung up his phone and quickly began to get dressed. He'd just gotten a call from one of his loyal Spades members informing him that they had the drop on Prince. "Get dressed baby. I just got the word on Prince," he called out. He had been waiting for a while to get his hands on Prince. To say he owed him one was an understatement.

Ivy lay on the bed already dressed. All she had to do was grab her gun and slip her shoes on. Wolf noticed that lately Ivy had been in a bad mood. It was like the more days that passed the worse her attitude was becoming. Wolf was doing his best to stay out of Ivy's way, but with the two shacked up in a room all the time it was kind of hard not to invade on the other's space.

"Did you hear me?"

Ivy sucked her teeth. "Yeah I heard you! You ain't got to yell!"

"I'm not yelling," Wolf said looking at Ivy like she was crazy. "I was just asking if you heard me because you didn't acknowledge me."

Ivy flicked her wrist and waved Wolf off. "You are always fussing about something..."

"What?"

Ivy hopped to her feet. "I said you are always fussing about something! DAMN!" she yelled. "Maybe you should try shutting up sometimes!"

Wolf didn't even realize that his hand had shot out in a blur and was around Ivy's throat. He forcefully shoved Ivy back up against the wall. "Listen to me carefully!" he growled. "I don't know what your problem is, but you better get it together and get it together fast!"

"Nigga you better take your motherfucking hands off me right now!" Ivy barked as she struggled to break free from his grasp, but it was no use. With no other options, Ivy raised her knee and kneed Wolf in the groin causing him to double over in pain. Out of natural reflexes, Wolf's hand shot out and smacked the shit out of Ivy. When he realized what he'd done he instantly regretted it.

"Baby I'm sorry! I didn't mean to..."

"Fuck you Wolf!" Ivy screamed as she went ballistic on him swinging wildly and trying to scratch his face all up. She couldn't believe that Wolf had put his hands on her. That was the one thing that he promised he'd never do.

"Baby I'm sorry," Wolf pleaded.

"You ain't sorry! I hate you!" Ivy yelled as she slipped on her combat boots, grabbed her 9mm from off the dresser, and then headed out the door leaving Wolf standing there.

CHAPTER 16

"Be Careful What You Ask For"

Wolf stood in the hotel room feeling stupid. His temper had gotten the best of him and he knew it. After Ivy left the room, someone from the lobby called up to, the room asking if everything was okay because someone had made a complaint about the noise. Wolf knew it wasn't safe for Ivy to be out of the room by herself, but his pride wouldn't let him go after her. He felt that she was wrong for speaking to him the way she had. Ever since Little Sunshine was murdered, Ivy hadn't been the same and neither had their relationship. It seemed like the harder Wolf fought for their relationship, Ivy fought even harder to ruin what they had worked so hard to build.

Wolf sat there for about six minutes debating on whether he should go after Ivy or not. After weighing the pros and cons he grabbed his twin Beretta's with the extended clips and headed towards the door. Wolf stopped dead in his tracks when he heard two loud gunshots ring out followed by the sound of a machine gun being fired. Seconds later the sound of screeching tires filled the air.

"Shit!" he cursed loudly as he flew out his room and headed downstairs as fast as he could. All Wolf could think about was Ivy. As he ran down the stairs he said a quick prayer. "Please God don't let nothing had happened to my baby!"

****

Ivy exited the hotel with tears running down her face. She couldn't believe how Wolf had just dealt with her. In Ivy's eyes, Wolf's actions showed her that he no longer loved her or had any type of respect for her and she refused to sit around and let a man put his hands on her. Yeah she loved Wolf, but sometimes you had to know when to let go. On her walk to the van Ivy realized that she was no longer good for Wolf. Her daughter couldn't be brought back and when Little Sunshine died a piece of Ivy died right along with her. It just hit Ivy that she was now just a shell of herself and Wolf deserved much more and right now she couldn't give it to him.

Ivy reached the van and just as she went to stick the key in the lock she heard footsteps approaching quickly from behind. Before she could do anything, she felt a strong hand clamp down on her shoulder.

"Bitch you coming with me!" the man wearing all black barked as he spun Ivy around so she was facing him.

Ivy spun around and jammed her 9mm in the pit of the man's stomach and fired off two shots.

POW!

POW!

Ivy watched as the man dressed in all black crumbled down to the ground. Innocent bystanders scrambled for safety. They were terrified that the next bullet may have their name on it. When Ivy looked up she saw several men dressed in all black holding assault rifles heading in her direction.

"Shit!" Ivy cursed. She tried to make her way to the driver side of the van, but the wounded man down by her feet; arm shot up and grabbed her shirt. Without thinking twice, Ivy turned and back slapped the wounded man across the face with the 9mm forcing the man to release his grip. She then quickly ran around to the driver side of the van and hopped behind the wheel just as another gunman opened fire on the van with a machine gun just as the van pulled out recklessly into the street.

"Shit!" Ivy cursed keeping her head ducked down as bullets ricochet loudly off the body of the van. She accidentally bumped and nudged a few cars as she did her best to try and stay alive. Ivy rested her 9mm on her lap and swerved from her lane to the incoming traffics lane and then back. She peeked in the rearview mirror and spotted four black Chargers in pursuit. With what started out as Ivy going out to get some fresh air and letting off some steam, turned into a shootout and then escalated into a high speed chase. Ivy reached down to grab her cell phone so she could call Wolf but quickly remembered she had left her phone on the charger plugged into the wall.

A black Charger pulled up on the driver side of the van and rammed into it, a move that the driver hoped would run Ivy off of the road. Ivy quickly snatched her 9mm from off her lap and fired three shots at the Charger's passenger window. The passenger window shattered as the driver hit the brakes no longer wanting to play the ramming game any longer.

Ivy made a sharp turn heading down a one way street. As she drove she reached down and touched her burning stomach and then raised her fingers up to her face to examine then.

Ivy almost went into shock when she saw that her fingers were covered in blood. "OH MY GOD!" she panicked. Paying more attention to her wound then the road, a car crashed into Ivy's van causing the van to break out into a fishtail. Ivy's van was then hit by multiple cars turning the van into a human pinball machine. Ivy's head slammed off the steering wheel and then everything got fuzzy and went black.

A man wearing all black quickly ran up and snatched Ivy's unconscious body from her van and roughly tossed her in the trunk of the Charger. Then he spun off leaving the smell of burnt rubber in the air.

CHAPTER 17

"The Real Is Back"

L ive Wire stepped foot in the packed club. Following close behind was Bills and four young cats who were dying to prove themselves to Live Wire. It had been around three to four months since the last time Live Wire was in a club. He was trying to cut back on the club scene, but tonight was different. Tonight the only reason him and his crew were in the club was because he had gotten word that Avon and his crew were in that exact club tonight. Live Wire wanted to talk to the man the streets called Avon face to face. Live Wire had heard that Avon was from out of town so he figured the way the man was moving, he must not have known who he was and how he got down. So tonight, Live Wire planned on introducing himself.

The club went wild when Lil Wayne's new song "Believe Me" came blaring through the speakers. As Live Wire tried to snake his way through the crowd, some big booty chick jumped in front of him and started twerking right in front of him. Live Wire was supposed to be in the club on business, but the freak in him just couldn't resist. He grabbed the chicks hips as his torso followed her ass to the beat. His crew egged him on as the chick bent down and grabbed her ankles while her ass moved like it had a mind of its own. Live Wire was about to do some freak shit and lift the chick up by her waist forcing her to do a hand stand with her legs still wrapped around his waist on the middle of the dance floor, but before he could make that move he felt someone forcefully grab his shoulder and spin him around.

Live Wire spun around and was standing face to face with Sparkle.

CHAPTER 18

"You Must Be Crazy"

Sparkle sat at the bar sipping on a Long Island iced tea. She had been in the house for the past week waiting for Live Wire to call her or show up to the house. After the big argument and the great make up sex, Sparkle hadn't heard from Live Wire. Tired of being stuck in the house all day, Sparkle decided to put on something sexy, go out, and stretch her legs. Needless to say she ended up in the club at the bar trying to drink away her problems.

Sparkle sat enjoying her drink when a guy sporting a fake Gucci hat with the matching fake belt approached her.

"What it do?" the man said with his breath smelling like garbage mixed with beer.

"Nothing," Sparkle said giving the man a look that said, *"get lost"*.

The man's eyes dropped down to Sparkle's ass. "Damn ma you looking like something," he said as he reached out for Sparkle's hand but she quickly snatched it back. "Come on baby don't act like that."

"Trust me I'm not acting!" Sparkle rolled her eyes and left the bozo in the fake Gucci standing there looking foolish. As

Sparkle snaked her way through the crowd in an attempt to get away from the fake Gucci man, she saw a crowd formed in the middle of the dance floor. Upon further review, Sparkle noticed that the man in the crowd dancing with some big booty chick was none other than...Live Wire! Sparkle was going to wait until the song finished before she interrupted the two, but she could no longer keep her composer when she saw the big booty chick drop down into a hand stand and wrap her legs around Live Wire's waist. *"Oh Hell Naw!"* Sparkle snapped as she pushed her way through the crowd and grabbed Live Wire's shoulder and spun him around. Immediately the big booty chick hopped up with an attitude

"Fuck is you doing?" the big booty chick snapped jumping in Sparkle's face. Live Wire quickly stepped in between the two women and escorted Sparkle over towards the bar before shit hit the fan.

"So instead of returning my calls, you rather be dancing with some hoe?" Sparkle yelled. "What happened to you? You were never like this!"

"Go home and I'll call you later," Live Wire said.

"Fuck you Live Wire! You don't tell me what to do no more!" she snapped. "You doing you and now I'm about to start doing me!"

"There you go hoe talking again," Live Wire said shaking his head with a disgusted look on his face. Usually he would have forced Sparkle to go home, but he was tired of fighting with her about the smallest things so he decided that it would just be best to let her go. "You wanna be a hoe, then go ahead," he said as him and his crew walked off leaving Sparkle standing there.

"Fuck you Live Wire! That's right go run back to your bitch on a string!" Sparkle yelled. "Go run to your whack ass bitch and when she leave you high and dry and take all your money, don't come back crying to me!"

Sparkle did her best to suppress the tears that were building up in the corner of her eyes. Never in a million years would she have thought that Live Wire would treat her like some side chick he'd just met. Sparkle wanted to go find Live Wire and scratch his eyes out, but she knew how that situation would play out if she did that.

"Fuck this shit," Sparkle said to herself. She was just about to head for the door when she felt someone grab her by the hand. She was about to tell whoever was grabbing her hand to kick rocks until she turned and saw a fine light skin brother with deep waves in his head standing before her.

"What's good love? Why you over here looking all sad?" the fine light skin man asked.

Sparkle shrugged. "Just going through a lot," she said honestly.

"Avon," the light skin man said extending his hand.

"Sparkle," she said accepting his hand.

"Come hang out with me and my crew tonight and put all your problems on the back burner just for one night," Avon said flashing his million-dollar smile. "I promise I won't bite, unless you ask me to."

Those words caused Sparkle to blush. At first she was going to decline the offer, but after giving it a second thought, she figured why not enjoy her night. Not only would she enjoy her night, but she could also piss Live Wire off all at the same time and to Sparkle that was a win, win.

CHAPTER 19

"At The Wrong Place At The Wrong Time"

After about thirty minutes of searching through the club, Live Wire and his crew were getting ready to call it quits. That was until one of Live Wire's henchmen pointed towards a crew that sat in the VIP section popping bottles over in the cut like it was nothing.

Live Wire and his crew made their way towards the VIP section when he saw Sparkle sitting next to one of the guys on the couch. As soon as Live Wire spotted Sparkle, his anger immediately began to rise.

Live Wire and his crew reached the VIP section and immediately he was met by Smokey and Kyra.

"Who you?" Smokey spoke.

"I'm Live Wire," he said with a smirk. "I would like to have a word with Avon."

"Fuck you wanna speak to Avon about?" Kyra barked jumping into the conversation.

"Bitch are you Avon?" Live Wire capped. "A'ight then shut the fuck up!"

Kyra took a threatening step forward, but stopped when Avon walked up.

"Come on in gentlemen and have a seat," Avon said welcoming Live Wire and his crew into the VIP area.

Live Wire, Bills, and his team stood. Live Wire looked over at Sparkle. "Get the fuck up outta here!"

Sparkle rolled her eyes and continued to sip from her drink. Right now Sparkle could care less what Live Wire was talking about. All she cared about at the moment was getting drunk and making Live Wire jealous. He was going to find out the hard way that it wasn't wise to play with a woman's heart. "I'm good," she said rolling her eyes and then crossed her leg over the top of the other.

"The lady's with me now," Avon said with a smile. "Now what can I help you gentlemen with?"

Live Wire ignored Avon. His glare was stuck on Sparkle. "Bitch I said you better get the fuck out of here... NOW!"

For a second, Sparkle was thinking about challenging Live Wire and telling him to kiss her ass, but when she saw the serious look on his face she decided to just leave in order to keep the peace. Sparkle stood up, kept her eyes on the floor, and exited the VIP section.

Once Sparkle was gone, Live Wire turned his attention back to Avon. "From what I'm hearing on the streets is that you are invading my territory."

"Your territory?" Avon chuckled. "Last time I checked it was a free country."

"Listen," Live Wire said trying to keep his composure. "You're invading my territory. There's rules to this shit."

"So what you saying? I can't get money?" Avon snapped.

"Yeah you can get money, but if you in my territory I'm going to have to tax you," Live Wire countered. Over the years he had put in an enormous amount of work to be able to have the power to decide who could and who couldn't get money.

"Listen," Avon spoke in a calm tone. "I'm not looking for any trouble, but if this situation was reversed would you pay taxes? Exactly," he said answering his own question. "Of course you wouldn't so don't expect me to pay either."

Live Wire had to admit he liked the young man's style and he admired his courage, but unfortunately this game had rules; rules that he planned on enforcing. "Either you pack up and move out on your own or I'm going to have to pack you up and move you out myself...Your call..."

"Who the fuck you think you talking to?" Kyra asked jumping into the conversation. She walked up and stood next to Avon like she was ready to do something.

Not liking how the chick came off or her tone of voice, Bills turned and stole on Kyra punching her dead in her mouth. From there a brawl broke out. Both crews clashed as bottles and chairs flew all over the place. In the midst of all the chaos, Live Wire had slammed Avon down to the floor and landed two punches to his face when Smoke jumped on Live Wire's back and threw him in a choke hold. Before things got too carried away the bouncers were able to separate both crews.

Outside Bills was ready to take things to the next level, but Live Wire quickly escorted him over to the car when he saw four cop cars pull up and park directly in front of the club.

"We'll save this for another day," Live Wire said as him and Bills hopped in different cars and exited the club's parking lot.

****

Live Wire was cruising down the highway when he heard his phone ringing. He looked down and saw Sparkle's name flashing across the screen. Just the sight of her name flashing across the screen instantly pissed him off. He wanted to rip her head off and bury it in some back woods somewhere. He quickly hit the ignore button as he pulled into Nikki's driveway and killed the engine. After a long day it felt good to come home to someone who truly loved and cared for him.

Live Wire stepped foot through the front door and saw Nikki laying across the couch wearing nothing but a black thong while reading a book.

As soon as Nikki heard the front door open, she jumped up and ran into Live Wire's arms.

"Oh my God baby I missed you so much!" Nikki said as she tried to squeeze the life out of Live Wire.

"How was your..." Nikki stopped in mid-sentence when she noticed a cut on the side of Live Wire's head. "You're bleeding," she said in a panicked tone. "What happened?"

"Nothing. It's just a scratch," Live Wire said trying to down play the seriousness of the situation.

"You went after that Avon guy didn't you?" Nikki asked already knowing the answer. "I know I can't tell you what to do, but just please be careful."

Live Wire was getting ready to reply but paused when he heard a loud knock at the door. He pulled his 9mm from the small of his back and then turned and faced Nikki. "You expecting company?"

Nikki quickly shook her head no.

Live Wire slowly made his way to the door and looked through the peephole. He then put his gun back down in his waistband as he opened the door and on the other side of the door stood Wolf.

CHAPTER 20

"Back Like I Never Left"

Live Wire stood and looked at Wolf for a long moment before he broke the silence. "What's good bro? Long time no see."

"I need your help," Wolf told him. He stood with a hoodie over his head, with his hands down in the pockets, and his hands resting on twin .45's.

"I heard what Pauleena did to your little one," Live Wire said in a sad tone. "Why didn't you come to me sooner? I mean I know we weren't fucking with each other but we're still family," he said stepping to the side so Wolf could enter.

"Sorry for just popping up like this."

"How did you find out where I was anyway?" Live Wire asked.

"I stopped by your old crib and just as I was about to leave, I saw Sparkle pulling into the driveway." Wolf smirked. "She gave me an ear full before finally telling me that you were over here with some new shorty."

Soon as the words left Wolf's mouth, Nikki emerged from upstairs covered in a black silk robe. "Baby is everything alright?" Nikki asked in a concerned tone. Instantly she recognized the man in the hoodie from seeing his picture all over the news about a year ago. All they talked about on the news was how dangerous this man was and now there he was standing in her living room.

"Yeah baby, let me introduce you to somebody," Live Wire said. "Baby this is my brother Wolf and Wolf this is my baby Nikki."

"Nice to meet you Wolf," Nikki said smiling and then turned and faced Live Wire. "Can I have a word with you for a second?"

Once the two were out of ear shot, Nikki spoke in a hushed tone. "Um what is he doing here?"

"That's my brother! What you mean?"

"I saw that guys picture all over the news about a year ago talking about he was armed and very dangerous," Nikki said.

"The news be lying," Live Wire said with a smile.

"This is not funny."

"I've been knowing Wolf since we were young thugs just running the streets," Live Wire told her. "If he's here because he needs my help, I'm going to help him."

"But I'm scared!" Nikki admitted. The man with the hoodie covering his head scared her and something about him just screamed trouble. "I'm scared he's going to get you killed by getting you mixed up in his mess."

"Baby..." Live Wire said in a pleading tone. "You're thinking too much."

Nikki shook her head. "He's wearing a hoodie in the summer time, but I'm thinking too much?"

Live Wire laughed, but on the inside he knew everything that Nikki was telling him was the truth, but at the same time he couldn't just turn his back on Wolf.

"Just promise me you'll be careful," Nikki said with her mouth, but her eyes said that she wished that Live Wire would just tell his friend to leave.

"I got you."

"I'll be upstairs if you need me." Nikki kissed Live Wire on the lips and then disappeared upstairs.

"Everything good?" Wolf asked.

"Of course," Live Wire replied as he grabbed a bottle of Ciroc and two glasses as him and Wolf walked over and sat on the couch. "Now what's going on?"

"They got Ivy," Wolf said as he poured himself a drink. "We had an argument and she stormed out of our hotel room," he paused for a second. "Apparently Pauleena and her crew had been staking out our hotel and when they saw Ivy by herself, they made their move."

Live Wire was about to reply, but held onto his words when he saw the tears falling from Wolf's eyes. He had never seen Wolf cry before so whatever was going on had to be serious. "We gonna get her back."

"No we not!" Wolf snapped. "They are going to kill her!"

"Don't talk like that," Live Wire said trying to stay positive. He knew how ruthless Pauleena was so more than likely if Ivy wasn't dead she would be soon.

"You still have a lot of Real Spades members?" Wolf asked.

"Of course I do," Live Wire smiled. "I'll round the troops up and we'll hit the streets first thing in the morning."

"Let's paint the streets red!"

CHAPTER 21

"Finally We Meet Again"

Pauleena sat in the sitting room of her mansion with a drink in her hand while a Chinese woman sat in front of her hard at work on her toes. After returning from Columbia, Pauleena had a lot to think about. Chico had offered her a way out, a fresh start and the decision was up to Pauleena. Yeah she liked Chico and would love to spend the rest of her life living in luxury, but the truth was, Pauleena was an action freak, the type of person that would get bored with just living a normal life.

Pauleena closed her eyes and took a deep gulp from her drink as she weighed her options. Olivia's song "Where do I go," hummed softly through the speakers helping to put her mind at ease. *"You got two choices"* she said to herself. *"Either move to Columbia and live happily ever after like a queen with Chico, or stay here in the states and get killed or sent to prison for the rest of my life, or possibly have Chico send a hit squad up here to kill me."* Pauleena didn't like any of her options, but moving to Columbia made the most sense.

Big Ock walked in and interrupted Pauleena's silence. "Boss, some Jamaican fuck just showed up talking about he needs a word with you."

Pauleena's face crumbled up immediately. "A Jamaican? Unannounced?"

Big Ock smiled. He was fresh out on bail and couldn't wait to earn his pay. "Yup, I think he said he's Bobby Dread's cousin or some shit like that."

"What you think about me moving to Columbia?"

"Columbia?" Big Ock repeated with a confused look on his face.

"The big bosses are saying I'm causing too much heat and putting too much unwanted attention on the family," Pauleena said. "They said if I make the papers one more time a hit squad is going to come up here and take me and anybody associated with me out."

"Damn!" Big Ock shook his head. "I was scared that it would come down to this... What are you going to do?"

Pauleena thought about it for a second before she replied. "I don't know yet."

"Just know whatever you decide to do, I got your back," Big Ock said meaning every word. To him Pauleena wasn't just his boss, she was family. She was the only family he'd ever had and whatever her decision was whether good or bad he planned on riding with her to the very end.

Pauleena smiled and then took another sip from her drink. Before she could say another word, another one of her Muslim bodyguards entered the sitting area and informed her and Big Ock that their guest was beginning to get impatient and upset.

"Send him in," Pauleena huffed as she finished her drink only to have her maid quickly give her a refill. She wasn't really in the mood for any guest nor did she have the energy to entertain foolishness at the moment. She had a few tough decisions to make, decision that would need her undivided attention. Pauleena sipped her drink as the Chinese woman removed her feet from the tub of water, dried them, and began to polish her toes.

Two minutes later a man with dread locks that ended near his calves entered the sitting area followed by Big Ock and four other Muslims dressed in suits and bowties.

"Who the fuck are you and why the fuck are you here unannounced?" Pauleena sipped her drink.

"The name is Tony," the man with the dreads said. "I'm Bobby Dread's cousin and me and the rest of the Yardie family don't like the way our brother Bobby Dread was treated after his death."

"Listen," Pauleena said sitting up in her seat. "I'm sorry about your loss. Bobby Dread was one of my best soldiers and his death hit me just as hard as you, but I know just like he knew that this is a dangerous business and sometimes you have to take the good with the bad."

"I understand that this is a dangerous business, but me and my peoples don't like how Bobby Dread was handled after he was murdered." Tony said with his voice full of anger. "The least you could of done was paid for his funeral since he died protecting you. Not even one person from your crew attended his funeral."

The truth was that as soon as Pauleena heard about Bobby Dreads death, Wolf and Ivy had made their move on her and then from there she'd spent the next two weeks in Columbia with Chico.

"Listen I understand that you and your people are upset but this has been a rough week for me," Pauleena told him. She understood what the man was saying. His timing was just bad. So instead of being disrespectful she decided that it would be best to postpone this conversation for another day. "Tell you what; why don't we set up a time and place to discuss all of this sometime next week?"

Tony looked at Pauleena like she had just spit in his face. "I come to talk to you about one of my fallen brothers and you tell me to my face that now is not a good time?" Tony snapped. "You disrespectful bitch!"

"What the fuck you just said?" Pauleena sat her glass down and stood to her feet.

"You are a disrespectful woman. I personally called you at least ten times last week just to see if you would come to the funeral," Tony said. "You and your organization have disrespected our family too many times. Now to show good faith me and my family request two million dollars... Cash."

A smirk danced on Pauleena's lips. She was about to wild out but caught herself as Chico's words echoed in her head. "So let me get this right. You came here to try and muscle me out of two million?"

"Pauleena it would be wise for you to just pay the money, cause trust and believe the last thing you want is a war with the Jamaicans. It wouldn't end pretty for you," Tony said showing no fear.

Pauleena looked over Tony's shoulder and gave Big Ock a private look. He quickly replied with a simple head nod.

"How long do I have to get the money to you?" Pauleena asked.

"You have one week. When your seven days are up and you haven't made a payment, we will take that as an act of war," Tony said. "My family won't tolerate this kind of disrespect especially not from a woman. In our country women are supposed to...." Immediately something crashed down on the back of Tony's skull causing his whole world to shake up. His vision went blurry and the most excruciating headache overcame him. Big Ock stood over Tony and delivered a kick to his ribs.

"You wanna come in here talking all this tough shit!?" Pauleena growled looking down at Tony.

"You're making a terrible mistake," Tony warned.

Pauleena kicked Tony in his face with her bare feet forcing his head to snap back. "Filthy ass Jamaican nigga come in here talking crazy!"

One of Pauleena's Muslim body guards walked over and handed her a thick chain, the type of chain that one would use to lock up his bicycle or the doors to a building. At the end of the chain rested four Master locks.

"Wait!" Big Ock said. "What about the Columbians?"

"Fuck the Columbians!" Pauleena yelled smiling as she drew the chain back and struck Tony with the chain like he was an animal. "You wanna come in my house talking crazy!?"

WHACK!

"Talking like you built like that!?"

WHACK!

"I better give you two million or else right!?"

WHACK!

"In your country women ain't shit right!"

WHACK!

WHACK!

"You gonna learn today motherfucker!"

WHACK!

WHACK!

WHACK!

WHACK!

WHACK!

"That's enough!" Big Ock stepped in and grabbed the chain from Pauleena's hand. "He's dead."

Pauleena walked over to the wet bar area and poured herself another drink. It wasn't until she took that first sip that she realized that she had just fucked up big time. She was already in hot water with the Columbians and now that Tony was dead, a war with the Jamaicans was sure to follow. *"Fuck,"* she said to herself. She had let her anger get the best of her.

Big Ock walked over and poured himself a drink and smiled.

"What's so funny?"

"You just dug our graves," Big Ock said. Him and Pauleena stared at each other for a second then broke out into a laughing fit.

"I couldn't help myself. That Jamaican fuck was asking for it," Pauleena said taking another sip.

"What's our plan from here?" Big Ock asked. "Pack up and disappear before shit hit the fan?"

Pauleena finished the rest of her drink in one gulp and then refilled her glass before she spoke. "Fuck that! I ain't going nowhere!" she spat. "On some serious shit, if you want to leave before shit hit the fan, I won't be mad with you... I understand you have a life of your own and may want to go and enjoy your money."

Big Ock finished his drink and then held out his glass so Pauleena could fill him back up. "If you ain't going nowhere, then I ain't going nowhere," he said then smiled.

"That's why I fucks with you," Pauleena said as she hugged Big Ock tightly. Nowadays it was hard to come across any loyal friends and she appreciated Big Ock for not leaving her out to dry like most people would have.

Pauleena took a sip of her drink and she watched as a few of her body guards got rid of Tony's body. Just as Pauleena was about to sit down and try to enjoy the rest of her night, she saw The Big Show, Prince, and a few other goons walking down the huge hallway with a battered and bruised woman in their possession.

"Brought you a present!" The Big Show said as he tossed Ivy towards Pauleena's feet.

At first, Pauleena didn't recognize the women that lay before her feet. With all the bruises and blood that covered her face, it took Pauleena a second or two before she realized that the woman that laid before her feet was none other than Ivy.

CHAPTER 22

"A Sticky Situation"

Ivy lay on the floor bleeding with her hands cuffed behind her back. Finally, she was face to face with the monster that murdered her daughter, but this wasn't how she imagined it playing out. She knew at the moment she had no wins and wished that she hadn't left Wolf's side. It wasn't until now that she realized that the way she had been treating Wolf was totally uncalled for and unnecessary, but now it was too late to go back and apologize.

"Well, well, well," Pauleena said interrupting Ivy's thoughts. "When I killed your daughter and let you keep your life I thought that I was doing you a favor." She paused. "But apparently some people don't know when to quit." She sipped her drink. "Now do they?"

"Fuck you!" Ivy growled. She refused to give Pauleena the satisfaction of hearing her beg for her life.

"Fuck me?" Pauleena repeated as one of her bodyguards handed her the same chain that she had just used on Tony. "You come in my house and disrespect me?"

"Fuck you!" Ivy spat again. "Just like a coward you'll kill me while I'm hand cuffed! Uncuff me and let's do this like real women!" she challenged.

Pauleena chuckled. "I would love to, but unfortunately right now I don't have time to play with you."

"Just like I thought! You ain't nothing but a punk bitch!" Ivy spat.

Pauleena smoothly walked over and kicked Ivy in the face. She then stood over Ivy and wrapped the thick chain around her neck and pulled tight. "What you said!? Say it again! I couldn't hear you!" Pauleena said as Ivy choked and gurgled trying to take a desperate breath. "Yeah that's what I thought!" Pauleena huffed as she stood up and punched Ivy in the face. Once the chain was removed from around Ivy's neck, she broke out into a coughing fit.

"Where's Wolf hiding?" Pauleena asked looking down at a battered and bruised Ivy.

"Fuck you!" Ivy coughed and then spit inches away from Pauleena's foot.

Pauleena gave Ivy a sad look and then shook her head. Without warning she quickly drew her arm back and swung the chain with force. She watched as Ivy squirmed when the chain made contact with her back. "What I told you about playing with me!"

WHACK!

"Come up in my house talking all this tough shit!"

WHACK!

"Like you don't know what I do for a living!"

WHACK!

"Tryna protect that bum ass nigga!"

WHACK!

WHACK!

WHACK!

WHACK!

When Pauleena got done she looked down at what was left of Ivy. "Put this bitch body somewhere that everyone can see it," she said breathing heavily. She then headed upstairs to her master bedroom to get some much needed rest that she so desperately needed. Pauleena would deal with her problems tomorrow. Tonight all she wanted to do was be alone and get some sleep. Once she was in her bedroom, she stripped down to her birthday suit and laid naked across her circular bed. As soon as Pauleena closed her eyes, the buzzing of her phone caught her attention. "Shit!" she cursed as she reached down and picked up her phone from the floor and saw Chico's name flashing across the screen.

CHAPTER 23

"Party Time"

L ive Wire parked his Benz in the parking lot of the strip club. Word on the street was the champion was in the building. Wolf had heard that over the years that The Terminator and Pauleena had gotten close over the last few years. The Terminator was the pound for pound best boxer on the planet at the moment. He was known for always being in the middle of some shit, having a lot of women, and not giving a fuck. Having no other choice, Wolf thought it would be a good idea to pay the champ a visit and see if they could get some information out of him. A van full of Live Wire's shooters pulled up and parked next to the Benz.

"Ya'll be on point just in case some shit jump off," Live Wire said to the driver of the van as him and Wolf placed their guns in the glove compartment of the Benz.

Live Wire and Wolf reached the front of the strip club and were immediately met by a huge bouncer. The two men were roughly frisked and patted down before they were allowed entry into the club.

A grin quickly spread across Live Wire's face when he saw all the ass that was jiggling all over the place. Over in the corner, a group of men roared when a thick stripper slid down the pole and broke down into a Chinese split, never missing a beat as she bounced her ass to the beat simultaneously.

"Stay focused," Wolf yelled over the music into Live Wire's ear. He could already see Live Wire's eyes beginning to wonder around staring at all the naked ass in the club.

"I'm good," Live Wire replied with his eyes never leaving the thick stripper's body that was on stage. He couldn't put his finger on it, but he could of sworn he'd seen the chick somewhere before. Live Wire's thoughts were interrupted when he saw Avon and his crew enter the strip club. What really pissed him off was who was with Avon. Live Wire's mood instantly turned dark when he saw Sparkle enter the club on Avon's arm.

"I found The Terminator," Wolf said as he noticed Sparkle enter the strip club with another crew that looked like they were getting money. "Let it go Live! We're here for business!"

Live Wire nodded, but Wolf could tell that his mind was now on Sparkle and her new friend. "I'm good," he said as him and Wolf headed over towards the section where The Terminator stood.

CHAPTER 24

"Make It Rain"

The Terminator stood with a handful of bills in both hands as a thick red bone chick gave him a fully nude lap dance. All the dancers were required to wear at least a thong, but when the champ was in the building certain rules went out the window. The Terminator tossed some dollars down on the woman's head and looked around to see if his entourage were enjoying themselves as well. All the strippers loved when The Terminator was in town. He was well paid and didn't have a problem spreading the wealth.

The Terminator stood up and tossed a handful of dollars out towards the stage. The champ was dressed in all black and around his neck hung three thick expensive looking chains. A chunky iced out bracelet decorated his wrist and he wore four rings on one hand just because he could. He looked through his dark tinted shades for two lucky strippers that could have the pleasure of sucking his dick for the night when he spotted a small commotion over towards his left. His security was in a heated conversation with a group of men wearing all black.

"Fuck going on over here?" The Terminator asked one of his security guards.

"These clowns talking about they need to have a word with you or else!" the security guard informed him.

The Terminator pushed his way to the front to see what was going on. "What's popping?" he asked looking at Wolf. He had seen the man somewhere before but couldn't quite pin point where or when.

"I'm looking for Pauleena. Do you know where I can find her?" Wolf asked.

The Terminator chuckled and then shook his head. "Looking for her is like looking for a death wish. If I were you, whatever problem you have with her, I would just leave it alone," he advised. He and Pauleena had become cool over the years and he was happy to call her a friend rather than an enemy.

"Motherfucker do you know where we can find the bitch or not!?" Live Wire barked.

"Who the fuck you think you talking to like that!?" a big security guard snapped as he roughly grabbed Live Wire. From there all hell broke loose. Live Wire fired off a quick two piece that hit the security guard square on his chin. The guard took the punches well and then grabbed Live Wire and rushed him back into the rail where the two men flipped over the banister falling down to the lower level of the club.

Instantly Live Wire's crew clashed with The Terminator's security team. Bottles and chairs went flying all over the place. In the mist of all the commotion, The Terminator snuck up on Wolf and stole on him knocking him out cold in the process before his security quickly escorted him out the club before any more damage could be done. The Terminator didn't know what was going on, but once he saw fist start to fly he got in where he fit in.

The Terminator's security team rushed him out of the club only to find some fat chick and a man with a pair of fake True Religion jeans sitting on the hood of the champs Lamborghini taking pictures and fronting like the car belonged to them. Without thinking twice, one of The Terminator's bodyguards roughly shoved the couple off the hood and cleared a path so the champ could smoothly get in his ride. The Terminator hopped behind the wheel of his sports car when the sound of machine gun fire could be heard echoing throughout the parking lot.

****

A Spades member helped Wolf up to his feet and helped usher him towards the door. Wolf's vision was a little blurry and he walked on shaky legs. He looked around looking for any signs of trouble when the sound of gunfire sounded off loudly coming from outside. Wolf stumbled outside and saw Bills and the van full of goons having a shootout with The Terminator's bodyguards.

Wolf had no idea where Live Wire was or if he was even okay and with all the people running around it was hard to tell who was who. As him and the goon trotted through the parking lot, Wolf saw a familiar face that he knew way to well.

Wolf spotted The Big Show and a few familiar looking Spades members standing off to the side as if they were just getting ready to enter the club when all hell broke loose. Once Wolf made it to the Benz, he snatched his .45 from the glove compartment and jogged in a low crouch over to where The Big Show and his crew stood.

CHAPTER 25

"Mr. Cool"

The Big Show stood off to the side as he watched people scramble for their lives. The sound of gunfire didn't scare him. He had been doing dirt for so long that it was now normal to him. The Big Show and The Spades arrived at the strip club in hopes to run into Avon. Word had got back to Pauleena that some new cat named Avon had called himself taking over shit in her city so she sent The Big Show down to the strip club to show the new jack how things really worked in New York.

The Big Show watched all the pandemonium with a smirk on his face. He lived for violence. He was just about to say something to the man standing next to him when a bullet exploded in his shoulder. The impact forced him to spin around. The Big Show stumbled backwards and then locked eyes with the shooter. He knew Wolf was in town, but hadn't expected to see him, especially not at the strip club. Four ex-Spades members dropped like flies as another bullet exploded in The Big Show's thigh forcing him down to the unforgiving concrete. He looked up and saw Wolf closing in on him.

****

Wolf walked up on The Big Show who lay helplessly on the ground. Just as he was about to put a bullet in his head, Wolf glanced over to his left and saw Live Wire making his way over, but creeping up behind him were two men with bad intentions in their eyes. Wolf recognized two of them from when they walked in with the guy who Sparkle was hanging out with.

"Shit!" Wolf cursed as he aimed him gun at the first gunman and took him out with a head shot. He dropped the next gunman with two shots to the chest. He quickly jogged over to where Live Wire stood and found him sprawled out on the concrete with blood everywhere.

"Where you hit at?" Wolf asked in a panicked tone as he kneeled down next to Live Wire.

"My hip and my lower back," Live Wire said wincing in pain. Wolf looked back at The Big Show and turned back to Live Wire. He helped Live Wire up to his feet and half carried him back to the Benz.

"Hang in there!" Wolf said as he zoomed out the parking lot just as the police showed up and joined in on the action. "I'll get you to the hospital in no time!"

"No I'm not going to no hospital!" Live Wire growled. "Take me home!"

"You need medical attention!" Wolf told him.

"Nikki's going to be a doctor soon. She'll know what to do," Live Wire replied.

CHAPTER 26

"Healing Wounds"

Nikki pranced around the house wearing a sexy black lingerie thong set and black fish net stockings covered her legs and thighs. She had just finished cooking dinner. Nikki usually wasn't the type of chick to wear sexy lingerie, but for Live Wire she was willing to be everything he needed and then some. So tonight she planned on feeding her man and then pleasing her man until he begged her to stop.

Nikki glanced down at her phone and began to get worried. She had texted Live Wire over an hour ago and still hadn't gotten a response. *"He always responds quickly to my text. I hope nothing is wrong,"* Nikki thought as she went to Live Wire's name in her phone. Just as she was about to send him another text, the front door came busting open and in walked Wolf carrying a bloodied Live Wire.

"Oh my God!" Nikki screamed as she covered her mouth with her hands. As soon as she saw all the blood, the first thing she thought was that Live Wire was dead.

Wolf quickly knocked all the food that Nikki had just cooked off the counter with a sweep of his arm. "Come give me some fucking help!" he yelled as he struggled to lift Live Wire up on the counter. Nikki wanted to help but for some strange reason she couldn't move. Her brain was telling her to move, but her body refused to respond. Finally Wolf got Live Wire up on the counter and when he did, he noticed he'd passed out. He looked over towards Nikki and saw that she had fainted. The sight of blood plus the thought that Live Wire was dead was just too much for her to handle.

"Shit!" Wolf cursed. The last thing he wanted to do was call an ambulance because if an ambulance arrived, the police were sure to follow. Having no other choice, Wolf ran over and grabbed Nikki's cell phone from off the floor and dialed 911. Wolf waited around until he could hear the sirens and then he disappeared into the night. He felt bad about leaving Live Wire like that, but he had to do what he had to do.

CHAPTER 27

"This My City"

Pauleena sat behind the wheel of her bullet proof Benz. Big Ock sat in the passenger seat as the two cruised through the city. Two SUV's full of Pauleena's Muslim bodyguards tailed closely behind her Benz. Pauleena was tired of being cooped up in the house all day. She had made up her mind that she was indeed going to take Chico up on his offer and move out to Columbia with the billionaire, but first she had to settle the unfinished business that she had with Wolf. This beef had been going on for way too long and Pauleena was ready to settle the score once and for all. "Is this clown legit?"

"He supposed to be," Big Ock replied as Pauleena pulled up in front of a ran down looking house.

Three big bodyguards hopped out of the SUV and ran over and opened the door to the Benz just as Pauleena stepped out. The bodyguards then surrounded Pauleena like she was the president as she made her way to the front door of the raggedy looking house.

Big Ock knocked on the door and waited patiently for an answer. An older man with salt and pepper hair answered the door. Big Ock wasted no time forcing his way inside the house. "Who else is in the house with you?" Big Ock asked as his placed the barrel to his P90 under the old man's chin.

"Just me and the good Lord," the old man said in a shaky voice. Seconds later Pauleena entered the house with a smirk on her face.

"You Roy?" she asked. The old man nodded his head yes.

"I was told you had some information for me on where I can find Wolf. Is this true?"

"Sho is," The old man smiled. "And for a couple of more dollars I can throw in Live Wire as well."

"And how do I know that your information is valid?" Pauleena asked with a raised brow.

"If it's not accurate, I give you permission to come back and kill me," the old man told her.

Pauleena smiled at the old man's answer because his life would surely be taken away if he made her pay for some bad information. "Pay the man," she said as she watched Big Ock hand the old man an envelope stuffed with money.

"As a matter of fact, I know where you can find Live Wire right now," the old man volunteered.

Pauleena smiled. "I'm listening."

CHAPTER 28

"A Shower Run"

Nikki stepped out of the shower and dried off quickly. She had spent the last two days in the hospital with Live Wire and she had come home to take a quick shower while he was taking a nap. While in the hospital, Nikki found herself arguing with a detective for handcuffing Live Wire's wrist to the rail of his bed. She didn't understand why Live Wire was being handcuffed when he was the one who had been shot. She wanted to get back to the hospital quickly before those sneaky detectives tried some funny business.

Nikki made her way downstairs and stopped dead in her tracks when she saw a house full of men dressed in suites standing in her living room. She thought about running back upstairs but a woman's voice quickly erased that thought from her mind.

"Take another step and I'll blow you out your shoes!" Pauleena yelled.

"What do you want?" Nikki asked doing her best to hide her fear.

"Do you know who I am?" Pauleena asked.

"No I do not know who you are, but I know you are a drug queen pin because I've seen you and your high priced lawyer on the news a few times," Nikki capped.

"So from what I hear you and Live Wire are an item now," Pauleena said smiling. "Where is he?"

"Why?" Nikki asked defensively.

"I would like to know so I can kill him," Pauleena answered.

"He's changed his entire life around. Why can't you just let him be?" Nikki asked. "I know he's done a lot of wrong in the past but he's a really good guy."

The living room immediately filled with laughter.

"You must not know Live Wire as well as you think you do," Big Ock said.

"Listen, I don't have time to play with you! Live Wire killed my mother! Now either you can tell me where I can find him or we can do this the hard way! You choose," Pauleena said as she removed the jacket to her skirt suit and slipped her hands in a pair of white latex gloves.

"Please," Nikki said as tears began to stream down her face. She knew whatever Pauleena had planned for her wasn't going to be good.

Pauleena gave Nikki a sad look and walked over and grabbed the iron that was sitting on the floor beside Big Ock. She plugged the iron into the wall. Nikki tried to take off running, but Big Ock quickly tackled her down to the floor.

"Listen whatever your name is, we're not here for you. Just tell us where Live Wire is and I'll let you go free," Pauleena said. "This is your last chance."

Nikki thought about giving up Live Wire's whereabouts, but she knew if she did, Pauleena would probably more than likely still kill her anyway so she said fuck it and remained silent.

"Strip this bitch!" Pauleena said as she grabbed the steaming hot iron and made her way over to where Nikkia lay pinned down. Nikki bucked and tried to thrust her hips upwards in an attempt to break free but it was no use.

Without warning, Pauleena pressed the hot iron against Nikki's stomach and listened to her skin sizzle.

"Arrrrrrrrgh!!!" Nikki screamed. "Aaaarrrrrgggh!" Each time Pauleena pressed the iron against Nikki's skin, it sounded like bacon frying in a pan.

"Last chance," Pauleena said looking down at a helpless Nikki.

"Please! Whatever Live Wire has done, he's sorry," Nikki pleaded.

Pauleena shook her head as she smashed the iron down on the side of Nikki's face. After a while Pauleena could no longer take the smell of the burning flesh. She stood to her feet, pulled out her .380, and blew Nikki's brains all over the carpet.

"Silly ass bitch!" Pauleena said as her and her team of bodyguards made their exit leaving Nikki's body behind to be found by the police.

CHAPTER 29

"Zero to One Hundred"

olf sat in the passenger seat of an all black minivan while Drake's song "0 to 100" hummed through the speakers at a low volume. At the moment his mind was all over the place. He hadn't seen or heard from Ivy since she had left the hotel that day. At first Wolf thought that not hearing nothing from Ivy was a good sign and that she was still alive, but when he got the call from one of his loyal Spades members claiming that he'd found Ivy, Wolf's heart leaped up into his throat.

"You alright boss man," Dre asked keeping his eyes on the road. Dre was one of the last Spades members that Wolf had personally handpicked a few years ago and until this day the young man still remained loyal.

"Yeah I'm good," Wolf lied. On the outside he seemed calm, but on the inside he was a nervous wreck. Just the thought of something happening to Ivy because of him was something that was sure to haunt him for a very long time.

Wolf took a swig from the open bottle of 1800 Coconut Tequila. For the past few days Wolf had really started to hit the bottle in an attempt to take his mind off of Ivy. On his lap rested his .45.

Dre pulled the minivan onto a quiet block, pulled over to the side of the street, pulled up a little further, and then killed the engine. Wolf hopped out the van with his gun in hand and immediately he spotted a few other Spades standing around with sad looks on their faces. He took a few more steps and stopped dead in his tracks. Immediately his eyes watered as tears quickly began to make their way down his face. Wolf didn't want to believe it, but it was hard not to. Up ahead, Wolf saw Ivy's decapitated head on the top of an abandoned car lying in a pool of blood. Wolf couldn't see it from where he was standing, but the rest of Ivy's body parts were chopped up and placed in the trunk of the abandoned car.

"Sorry you had to see it like this, but I knew you would have wanted to identify the body yourself," a tall Spades member that went by the name of Mario said.

Wolf remained silent for a few minutes and just took in the graphic scene. A part of him couldn't believe that Ivy was really dead, but another part of him had already assumed the obvious. "Who did this?" Wolf asked as he walked over and glanced down into the trunk where the rest of Ivy's chopped up body was placed.

"We found this in the trunk next to Ivy's body," Mario said handing Wolf a folded up piece of paper.

Wolf took the paper from Mario, unfolded it, and began to read the note.

Play time is over Wolf. I'm coming for you next. This city ain't big enough for the two of us so why don't we settle this like G's.... I'll be seeing you soon!

Yours Truly: The Queen Pauleena

Wolf crumbled up the note, tossed it over his shoulder, and then turned to Mario. "Any idea where I can find this bitch?"

"We have to go after her money," Mario said. "Hit her pockets and that will surely bring that bitch out of hiding."

Wolf massaged the bridge of his nose. "What did you have in mind?"

"Attack all of her businesses and that's how you'll get to her." Mario paused. "This thing between you two has gone too far. It's now time for it to come to an end."

Wolf nodded his head. Mario was right. This beef between him and Pauleena had been going on for way too long and it was now time to end this once and for all. He had lost a lot ever since he decided he was going to do something about her poisoning the community with drugs.

"I heard she's got a nice low key lounge a couple of blocks from here," Mario said with a smirk on his face. "You wanna stop by and see how the customer service is?"

"Let's do it!"

CHAPTER 30

"Don't Play With Me"

The minivan pulled up in front of the lounge and Wolf quickly hopped out the van followed by several Spades members. Wolf walked towards the entrance when he was stopped by two beefed up bouncers.

"Sorry fellas but you're not wearing the proper attire for me to allow you in here," the bouncer said in a deep strong voice.

Wolf ignored the big man and fired a bullet into his thigh. The other bouncer tried to take off in a sprint, but a bullet to his lower back stopped him dead in his tracks. A Spades member stood outside with the bouncers to make sure they didn't call the police and to make sure no one else entered the lounge while Wolf and the rest of The Spades entered the lounge.

Wolf stepped foot inside the lounge and looked around. What he saw were happy people dancing, drinking, and enjoying themselves. He raised his .45 over his head and fired four shots up into the ceiling. Immediately the music stopped and everyone stampeded towards the exit. Wolf turned his attention to the bartenders and noticed that one was reaching for something. Before he could even react, the bartender was quickly shot down by two Spades members.

Wolf calmly walked over towards the bar. "Vodka and orange juice please," he said in a calm tone as he watched one of the bartenders fix his drink and then hand it to him.

Wolf took a sip of his drink. "Would any of you happen to know where I can find Pauleena?"

The three remaining bartenders all shook their head no in unison.

Wolf took another sip and then reached over the counter and smacked the shit out of one the bartenders. He slapped the woman so hard that she hit the floor. He then hopped over the counter and snatched the woman up to her feet by her hair and jammed his gun up under her chin. "Bitch you got three seconds to tell me something or else I'm going to blow your motherfucking brains out!" he growled.

The bartender looked Wolf dead in his eyes and said, "fuck you I ain't telling you shit!"

Wolf pulled the trigger and watched the woman's brains pop out the top of her skull like a jack in the box. He then made his way over to the next bartender in line and jammed his gun under her chin. "You got three seconds to tell me something!"

"Okay, okay, I'll tell you what I know. Just please don't shoot me," the bartender pleaded.

The bartender next to her quickly jumped in. "No Cathy! Don't tell them shit! You know what's going to happen..." She was quickly silenced with a bullet to the head.

Wolf then turned back to Cathy. "Spill it!"

"I've never met Pauleena, but I've heard all about her," Cathy said. "If something ever went wrong here, our orders are to call Prince," she told him.

"Where can we find him?" Wolf asked.

"I know where one of his houses are," Cathy said. "One of the bartenders here used to mess around with Prince a while ago and one day she asked me to give her a ride over there. I dropped her off at a big house in a quiet neighborhood."

"Do you mind taking me to this house?" Wolf asked.

"I'll do whatever you need me to do. Just please don't kill me," Cathy pleaded.

"You got my word that I won't kill you," Wolf replied.

CHAPTER 31

"I'm Out Here"

Pauleena's Benz pulled up in front of a project building. She knew she wasn't supposed to be dead smack in the middle of the hood, but she wanted the people to see her face, to feel her presence, and to know that she still was the queen. Pauleena stepped foot out of the Benz and was immediately surrounded by several Muslim bodyguards in suits. Her heels clicked loudly against the concrete with each step she took drawing the attention of all the hustlers and local thugs that stood around loitering.

"Oh shit that's Pauleena right there," she heard one of the local thugs say to the rest of his buddies as she walked pass.

A crowd of men stood in front of the building that Pauleena was headed to. The men quickly spread like the Red Sea and made a path. The men acknowledged Pauleena with a head nod as her and her security entered the building.

Pauleena and her security piled on the elevator and rode until it stopped on the requested floor. Big Ock stepped off the elevator and banged on the first door to his left. Seconds later a slim guy with fuzzy cornrows answered the door with a blunt hanging from between his lips. When he realized who was at the door, he quickly snatched the blunt from his mouth and stood straight up.

"Hey come on in," the guy said as Big Ock shoved him out of the way and entered the apartment.

Pauleena stepped foot in the apartment and saw The Big Show sitting in a wheelchair with a blunt in his mouth and a bottle of Hennessy sitting on his lap. He smelled like shit mixed with alcohol. The rugged beard on his face told Pauleena that he hadn't shaved in over a week or two.

"Fuck you doing here?" The Big Show slurred as he took a long drag of the blunt that hung between his lips.

"What happened to you?" Pauleena asked.

"Ran into our old friend Wolf," The Big Show said and then lifted the bottle to his lips and took a deep swig. "And now here I am," he said nodding down towards the chair.

"So you take a few bullets and that's it, you quit?" Pauleena asked as she plucked the bottle from The Big Show's hands and took a swig.

"Fuck you!" The Big Show growled. "We killed the man's wife and kid! Now he's on an expected rampage and for the record, I didn't quit, but when you live by the gun you die by the gun," he said in a defeated tone as he banged his fist against the chair out of frustration.

"You gonna be alright. I'll hire you the best doctor and hopefully..."

"My fucking dick doesn't even work anymore," The Big Show said cutting Pauleena off. "I can't even please a woman anymore," he said as a tear escaped his eye.

"I promise I'll make Wolf pay for what he did," Pauleena promised.

"Please do," The Big Show said as he took a final drag from the blunt and then flicked it across the room. "Got word on that new jack Avon," he said with a smirk. "Word is, it's his birthday and he's supposed to be partying at that wild ass club downtown."

"The club that you and Prince got kicked out of that last time?"

"Yup."

"I need a favor," The Big Show said with a smile on his face.

"What's up?"

The Big Show grabbed a 9mm from off the table, cocked a round into the chamber, and held the gun out towards Pauleena. "Take me out of my misery."

Pauleena look at The Big Show and chuckled. "Fuck outta here! Don't play like that!"

"Does it look like I'm playing?" The Big Show asked as tears fell freely from his eyes.

"You bugging," Pauleena said. "You're going to be fine. I'm going to hire the best spine specialist out there and get you fixed back up."

"Can't no specialist fix me!" The Big Show barked. "The only person that can fix me is you!" He held the gun out towards Pauleena again. Pauleena reluctantly took the gun from The Big Show's hand.

"Fix me Pauleena; please," The Big Show begged. Pauleena walked behind The Big Show and rubbed his shoulders and placed the gun to the back of his head.

"I want you to know that I appreciate everything that you've done for me. You're a good man and I promise you I'll make Wolf pay for this," she whispered in The Big Show's ear as she pulled the trigger.

POW!!

"I'll have somebody here in thirty minutes to clean this mess up," Pauleena said to the man with the fuzzy cornrows as she and her team made their exit leaving The Big Show slumped over in his wheel chair with blood and brain matter running out of the back of his head.

Pauleena exited the building and hopped back behind the wheel of her Benz. A part of her felt bad about putting The Big Show to sleep, but the other part of her understood. If she was in the same situation, she probably would have wanted someone to pull her plug too.

"You alright?" Big Ock asked. He could sense that something was bothering her.

"I'm good."

"What's our next move?"

Pauleena smiled. "I feel like partying. Don't you?"

"I'm always up for a good party," Big Ock said as the Benz quickly pulled away from the curb.

CHAPTER 32

"Happy Birthday"

Avon and his crew sat in the V.I.P. section of the club. Most of his crew was out on the dance floor having a good time, but not Avon. He sat on the couch with a bottle of Ciroc in his hand and Sparkle sitting next to him. His eyes constantly scanned from left to right for any signs of trouble. Word on the streets was, he had finally popped up on Pauleena's radar and she planned on paying him a nice visit. That's why Avon paid the bouncers at the front door two thousand dollars to let him and his crew enter the club with their guns. Avon's motto was, it was better to be safe than sorry and tonight he planned on being safe.

"Loosen up baby. It's your birthday," Sparkle yelled over the loud music that blasted through the speakers as she stood up and seductively began to gyrate her hips in front of him. "Come dance with me baby." For the past month, Avon and Sparkle had been spending almost all of their time together and they had now become a couple. Avon was nowhere near the type of guy that Live Wire was, but he was easy on the eyes and he was getting money so Sparkle looked pass all of his flaws.

"I'm good baby. You go dance without me," Avon said taking a sip from his bottle. "I'll come join you in a minute," he lied.

"You suck," Sparkle said as she spun on her heels and made her way to the dance floor.

Once Sparkle was out of earshot, Kyra helped herself to a seat next to Avon. "I don't trust that bitch."

"Who, Sparkle?"

"Something ain't right about her," Kyra said.

"She's cool," Avon said defending her. "You thinking too much."

"Just keep a close eye on her," Kyra said as she got up and joined Smoke who sat two couches down from Avon.

Avon took a swig from his bottle as he saw flashing lights towards the entrance. Immediately everyone in the clubs head turned toward the entrance to see what all of the ruckus was about. Minutes later, The Terminator entered the club surrounded by several seven feet tall bodyguards. Avon watched as the crowd immediately surrounded The Terminator. The crowd partied and paid attention to the champs every move. A camera crew followed The Terminator as well. He was quickly escorted up to a V.I.P. section. Immediately several waitresses headed over to the champs V.I.P. section carrying bottles with sparkles attached to the top of them. Women from all races broke their necks trying to get into the champs V.I.P. section. Minutes later, there was another scuffle at the entrance. Avon craned his neck trying to see what was going on when he saw Pauleena enter the club with her team of Muslim bodyguards.

****

Pauleena stepped in the club and a smile instantly crept on her face. It had been a long time since she had been to such a hood club. Big Ock grabbed Pauleena's hand as he pushed his way through the crowd. Mr. Vegas classic "Heads High" came blasting through the speakers and immediately everyone went crazy. As Pauleena snaked her way through the club, she notice a light skin shirtless muscular man two stepping his way towards her. The light skin man reached out and grabbed Pauleena's hand and gently pulled her towards him.

Pauleena willingly met the man half way as their hips began to sway to the beat. Big Ock and the rest of Pauleena's bodyguards stood around and watched as she and the stranger got their freak on in the middle of the dance floor.

The light skin man gripped Pauleena's ass with both hands and held her close. Pauleena wrapped her hands around the light skin man's neck while looking him in his eyes letting him know that on the dance floor as well as in the bedroom she was a beast. Pauleena spun around and pushed her ass back into the man who was grinding on her backside. His genitals were practically resting in the crack of her ass. Pauleena bounced her ass like she was a professional stripper, forcing the light skin man to hold on for dear life. Once the song was over, the light skin man slapped Pauleena on the ass, turned his focus on another chick, and proceeded to give her the business.

Pauleena smiled as she followed Big Ock through the club. She had only been in the club for a few minutes and her forehead was already covered in sweat. Before she could take another step, a man wearing a red bandana on his head approached Pauleena.

"What's good ma? You trying to do something when the club let out?" the man asked flashing a mouth full of gold teeth.

Pauleena looked at the guy like he was crazy. "Fuck is you on Molly or something?"

"I got whatever you need baby," was the thug's response. Out of nowhere one of Pauleena's bodyguards stole on the thug and knocked him out for wasting their boss' time.

Pauleena kept on moving throughout the club as if nothing had even happened. She was there for one reason and one reason only. Her only reason was to find Avon.

Pauleena spotted a group of men in the V.I.P. section acting as if money wasn't an issue. She hadn't seen Avon face to face, but she was sure that had to be him and his crew over in the V.I.P. section. Pauleena leaned over and whispered in Big Ock's ear.

"I think that's Avon over there. I need you to go check it out for me," she told him.

Big Ock nodded and headed over towards the V.I.P. section alone. He reached the entrance to the V.I.P. section and was immediately met by three hard faced goons.

"Fuck you think you going?" a tall man with a long beard barked.

"I need to have a word with Avon," Big Ock said politely.

Smoke quickly stepped up. "Listen fam, take ya bowtie and bean pies and get the fuck up outta here before you get hurt."

"I come in peace. I'm just asking to have a word with Avon," Big Ock repeated.

"I think you misunderstood what I just said," Smoke sighed loudly. "Please leave before you get hurt," he said and then shoved Big Ock back a few steps.

"Tell Avon that Pauleena isn't going to like this." Big Ock smiled, then turned, and walked away. When Big Ock made it back over to where Pauleena stood, he relayed the message. Pauleena smiled and turned to her second in charge, a Muslim that went by the name of Rodney. "As soon as I walk out this door, I want you to air this whole shit out. Tear this place up," she ordered as Big Ock escorted her out of the club.

****

As soon as Rodney saw Pauleena step foot out of the club, he made his move. He pulled his Tech-9 out and him and rest of Pauleena's bodyguards headed over towards the V.I.P section.

****

Avon sat in the V.I.P. with Sparkle on his lap. She held a drink up to his lips when the sound of gunfire erupted. Immediately everyone hit the floor in an attempt to avoid getting struck with a stray bullet. Avon looked up and saw his team returning fire. He quickly grabbed Sparkle's hand and rushed her towards the side exit. Avon and Sparkle spilled out the side exit where two more men with suits and bowties stood waiting for them.

"Shit!" Avon cursed as him and Sparkle quickly dashed behind a parked car. Bullets pinged loudly off the car's body as broken glass rained down on top of their heads. Avon removed his 9mm from his waistband and returned fire just to keep the shooters at bay. Once the shooting ceased, Avon took off running leaving Sparkle behind to fend for herself.

He fired three reckless shots over his shoulder before hopping a fence and then disappearing around the corner.

Once the shooters saw Avon hop the fence, they took off after him. When the coast was clear, Sparkle took off her heels and took off running in the opposite direction.

CHAPTER 33

"Welcome To Hell"

"That's the house right there," Cathy said pointing to an expensive looking house. "That's the house that I dropped my home girl off to when she was going to meet Prince."

Wolf looked at the house and everything about it had Prince's name written all over it; from the fancy cars parked out front to the loud music that could be heard from a block away. "You did good," Wolf told Cathy. "I'll have one of my men take you home."

Once Cathy was out of the way, Wolf and his team of Spades soldiers crept towards the front of the house while a few other soldiers made their way around the back and searched for a back door.

On the silent count of three, Wolf aimed his shotgun at the door and blew the door off the hinges.

****

Prince sat on a stool over by the bar area of his home while Jim Jones' new mix tape blared through the speakers.

He was shirtless with a bottle of Grey Goose in his hand. Prince wore a pair of basketball shorts, some Nike slides, and a pair of Ray Bands covered his eyes while he entertained his guest. Prince invited a few of his best soldiers over along with some of the finest strippers he could find all in the name of having a good time. He smiled as he watched his soldiers have the time of their lives. He knew he wasn't paying them what they were supposed to be paid so every now and then he did something nice to show them how much he appreciated them.

"Why you over here acting all antisocial?" a stripper that went by the name Bubbles asked as she plucked the bottle of Grey Goose from Prince's hand and took a deep swing as she curled down on Prince's lap.

"Just chilling," Prince shrugged. The truth was, he had a lot on his mind. He had heard what Wolf had done to The Big Show and he knew that a big war was sure to follow.

"Anything I can do to take your mind off of your problems?" Bubbles said while slipping her hand down Prince's shorts as she began to fondle his manhood. "And I do mean anything…"

Prince put the bottle up to his lips and took a deep gulp. Then he removed his shorts and boxers. He quickly grabbed the back of Bubbles head and guided it down towards his dick. Once her face was close enough, he roughly jammed his dick in her mouth causing her to gag a little. Prince threw his head back and let out a low moan just as he heard the front door getting blown off the hinges.

Prince roughly shoved the stripper off him and ran for his gun that sat over on the coffee table, but a bullet to the back of his calf stopped him in mid-stride.

Wolf walked in the house and watched as The Spades shot up the entire house. The old Wolf would have felt sorry for the women in the house, but the new Wolf was numb to everything. He no longer had mercy for people or felt sorry for them. Losing your entire family could do that to a man. Wolf walked over and flipped Prince over on his back with his foot.

"Where's Pauleena?"

"Fuck you!" Prince spat defiantly. Wolf quickly raised his foot and brought it down hard across the bridge of Prince's nose breaking it instantly.

"Pick this motherfucker up!" Wolf ordered. He was tired of playing with Pauleena and her crew. It was time to let them know that he meant business. Two Spades forcefully sat Prince in a chair and bounded his hands behind his back and his ankles together. Another Spades member then handed Wolf a canister of gasoline.

Wolf splashed gasoline all over Prince's head and naked body then he struck a match. "You got something you want to tell me?" he asked with a raised brow.

Prince smiled. "Pauleena is going to kill you just like she did your daughter and that whack ass bitch you called your wife!" he said as he laughed loudly. "Fuck you and The Spades! All of y'all can kiss..."

Wolf tossed the match at Prince and watched as his body engulfed in bright orange and blue flames. Wolf stood there and listened to Prince's blood curdling screams and he watched as his body burned for a minute or two before he finally turned and left the house. He still didn't know where to find Pauleena, but he was weakening her armor each time he eliminated one of her soldiers. *"Bobby Dread down, The Big Show down, Prince down, and Pauleena you're next!"* Wolf said to himself as he slipped in the back of the van.

CHAPTER 34

"You're A Clown"

Sparkle hopped out the cab and walked towards Avon's house barefoot. She still couldn't believe that he had just left her for dead like that back at the club. The truth of the matter was that she could have been badly hurt or even worse, she could have gotten killed. *"I can't believe this nigga,"* she said to herself. The further she got to the house, the stupider she felt for allowing herself to get caught up with Avon to begin with. Sparkle removed her key from her purse and let herself in the house. The first thing Sparkle saw when she entered the house was Avon and a few of his friends sitting around drinking and talking shit like nothing had ever happened.

Sparkle cleared her throat loudly and grabbed everyone's attention. "Helloo! Remember me?" she said looking at Avon.

"Oh you made it," Avon said in an uninterested tone and then turned back around to finish his drink and conversation.

"Yes I made it, no thanks to you!" Sparkle snapped. "How could you just leave me like that?"

Avon and his boys laughed loudly. "Fuck you wanted me to do? Take a bullet for you?"

"No! I expected you to protect me like a real man is supposed to do!" Sparkle barked.

"Bitch please!" Avon sipped his drink and let out a strong laugh. "As a matter of fact, give me my key back. I don't even know why I gave you a key to begin with."

Sparkle reached down in her pocketbook like she was digging for her key, but instead pulled out a gun and aimed it at Avon's head. "Fuck you; you bitch ass nigga!" she yelled. "If I see anybody reach for anything, I'm going to blow his head off!" she barked.

"You making a big mistake," Avon said through clenched teeth. The last thing he ever expected was for Sparkle to be aiming a gun at his head.

Sparkle held the gun at Avon's head with one hand and quickly dialed a number on her cell phone with her other hand. "Yeah daddy it's me. Come on, we waiting for you," she said then ended the call. Seconds later Live Wire entered the house with a slight limp. He still wasn't one hundred percent healed, but he wouldn't miss an opportunity like this for the world. Behind him was his main man Bills and about ten goons dressed in all black wearing hoodies.

"How did I do daddy?" Sparkle asked with a smile.

"You did great baby," Live Wire said as he kissed Sparkle passionately right in front of Avon.

"I knew you wasn't nothing but a hoe!" Avon yelled. Just the thought of him getting played made him even more furious.

"I asked you nicely to just pay taxes," Live Wire said shaking his head sadly. "And you couldn't even do that."

"Fuck you and that hoe!" Avon growled. "Do what you gotta do!"

Without hesitation, Live Wire raised his arm and blew Avon's head off. Immediately Bills and the rest of the goons opened fire on the rest of Avon's crew leaving no witnesses.

"Oh my God, I'm so glad this is over," Sparkle said as she hugged Live Wire tightly. "I was so tired of faking like I liked Avon," she admitted. "You better not ever doubt my love for you!"

"Thanks baby," Live Wire said and then kissed Sparkle on the lips.

"Thanks my ass!" Sparkle snapped. "I did my part in setting Avon up. Now you do your part and get rid of that bitch Nikki!"

Live Wire's whole mood suddenly changed from happy to sad. "Nikki's dead."

"Are you serious?" Sparkle asked in shock. Of course, she didn't care for Nikki because of her relationship with Live Wire but she didn't want the girl to get killed. "That's fucked up."

"I don't want to talk about that right now. Let's just go home and enjoy the rest of our night," Live Wire said as Sparkle helped him in the passenger seat of his B.M.W.

"I got a few things I've been dying to do to you." Sparkle licked her lips and pulled away from the scene of the crime.

CHAPTER 35

"Fuck You"

Pauleena sat upstairs in the back office of her club counting money. She was a silent partner of one of the hottest nightclubs in New York and with the amount of heat that was on her, it was best that she remained just that; silent. She had hired a young Italian man by the name of Rick to be the face of the company. Pauleena had a few of her workers selling cocaine and pills all throughout the club. Of course the Italian man had a problem with it, but what was he going to do? He couldn't tell Pauleena how to run her own club?

"Everything good?" Big Ock asked looking down at the packed dance floor from the big one way window in the office.

"Yeah we straight," Pauleena said dropping the last stack of money in a duffle bag. Then she tossed the bag to Big Ock. She had heard about how Wolf and his peoples had been going around trying to destroy all of her businesses so she decided to beef up the security at the club just to be on the safe side.

Just as Pauleena and Big Ock were getting ready to leave they heard a knock at the door. Big Ock quickly checked to see who it was and then he turned and faced Pauleena. "It's Rick."

"Let him in."

"Hey Pauleena is everything okay? I noticed we have doubled the security in here tonight," Rick asked in a nervous tone. He knew what Pauleena did for a living and he knew about her reputation. He didn't want any of that foolishness near the club but what was he going to tell her?

"Yeah everything is good," Pauleena said. "You worry about the club and let me worry about everything else," she told him as she looked out the window down at the dance floor. "The place has been doing good I see."

"It's been doing very good actually," Rick said smiling.

"Keep up the good work," Pauleena said as she pinched Rick's cheek and left him standing there. "I'll call you tomorrow," she yelled over her shoulder as the rest of her security met her in the hallway and immediately surrounded her. Big Ock and the rest of her bodyguards escorted her out of the club.

Pauleena stepped outside and noticed that it was pouring down raining. Big Ock quickly opened up an umbrella and held it over her head as he walked her to the driver side of her cocaine white Benz. Once she was behind the wheel, Big Ock hurried over to the passenger side and hopped in.

Pauleena made the Benz come to life with a turn of the key and instantly the windshield wipers worked overtime as Trey Songz voice hummed through the speakers at a respectable volume. Pauleena pulled out from in front of the club and cruised down the street. As she drove, she began to think about Chico. Pauleena missed him. She missed being in his presence, missed his touch, and missed the company of a man period.   Pauleena hated to have to hear Chico's mouth, but at the end of the day everything he said to her was right and she realized he was just trying to look out for her in the long run.

"What you over there thinking about?" Big Ock asked.

"Chico," Pauleena admitted honestly. "We need to try to start keeping a low profile out here before Chico and the big bosses make good on their threats."

"We gonna be good," Big Ock said. "I think it might be a good idea to just leave and go to Columbia and never come back. A new location and scenery may be a good thing."

"But Columbia though," Pauleena said sucking her teeth. "Shit, I may have to convince Chico to move to Paris, Miami, Brazil, Mexico, or somewhere nice."

Big Ock laughed. "Yeah I guess Columbia is kind of a dry place to live."

"We'll figure it out," Pauleena said as she stopped at a red light.   Before Pauleena could say another word, four cars came out of nowhere and boxed her Benz in.   Several Jamaicans hopped out the cars holding A.K.'s and opened fire on Benz.   The bullets bounced off the bullet proof Benz. When Pauleena brought the vehicle, she made sure it was bullet proof and it came with run flat tires.   Even though the car was bullet proof, Pauleena still moved her head out of reflex when the bullets bounced off of the windows. Pauleena looked through her rearview mirror and saw the rest of her bodyguards return fire on the Jamaicans turning the once one sided gun battle into an old fashion shoot out.

A man with long filthy looking dreadlocks that came down to his ass hopped up on the hood of the Benz and squeezed down on the trigger of his A.K. sending bullets ripping into the windshield.

Pauleena quickly stomped down on the gas pedal forcing the Jamaican to summersault off of the hood of her car into the air like a rag doll. She rammed the Benz into the car that blocked her path. After ramming the car three times, the Benz finally cleared a path. As Pauleena flew pass all the carnage, three Jamaicans stood in her path. Each one of them aimed a machine gun at the Benz and opened fire. Pauleena punched down on the gas and ran through the three men as if they were invisible. Bodies bounced off of her windshield left and right.

"Damn! How many of these motherfuckers are there!?" Big Ock asked. It seemed like more cars filled with Jamaicans were pulling up back to back with each second that passed.

Just as the Benz found a clear path a wild looking Jamaican ran and jumped on the roof of a parked car and leaped and landed on the roof of the Benz just as it pulled off.

"Shit!" Pauleena cursed as she looked through the rearview mirror and saw four Jamaicans on motorcycles in pursuit. She quickly gunned the engine and made a sharp right turn down the ramp that led to the highway. Pauleena smoothly removed her .380 from her purse, opened the sunroof, and pumped three shots into the mid-section of the Jamaican that was glued to the roof of her car. She watched through her rear view mirror as his body hit the ground like a rag doll and get ran over by oncoming traffic. She then looked over to Big Ock. "Get these niggas off our ass!"

Big Ock reached under his seat and removed a tech-9, rolled his window down, stuck his arm out the window, and opened fire.

Through the rear view mirror Pauleena saw two men with dreads fly off their motorcycles and hit the ground hard. She smiled as she zipped in between cars weaving in and out of traffic. Pauleena looked down at the speedometer and saw that it read 97 mph. She looked over and saw Big Ock hanging half way out the window with his machine gun roaring loudly in a constant rhythm. It seemed like the more Jamaicans that Big Ock dropped, five more showed up out of nowhere.

"Step on it!" Big Ock yelled as he counted at least twenty-five gunmen on bikes speeding up on the Benz. He quickly ducked down in his seat and rolled the window back up as a motorcycle pulled up on the side of him. The rider looked straight ahead while the passenger held on tight with one hand and opened fired on the Benz with the other hand. "There's too many of them," Pauleena said peeking through the rear view mirror noticing that her men were nowhere to be found. If she had to guess, they were more than likely dead. She quickly cut the steering wheel to the right and hit the motorcycle knocking both men off the bike. They hit the ground hard and rolled across the cement like rag dolls.

Again Pauleena ducked her head down out of reflexes as the sound of bullets pinged loudly off the body of the Benz. "Give me your phone!" she yelled out. Once Pauleena had the phone in her hand she did something she told herself she would never do... she dialed 911.

"Fuck is you doing!?" Big Ock asked.

"We need help!" Pauleena yelled as she looked in the rearview mirror and saw even more motorcycles in pursuit. The constant sound of bullets tearing into the Benz made it sound like a marching band was behind them. "911 yes I'm being attacked on the highway. Please send help now!" she said then ended the call. All she could do now was keep on driving until the cops showed up. Pauleena ran as many motorcycles off the road as she could, but there was just too many of them. Just when it looked like it was going to be all over, Pauleena heard sirens. She'd never been so happy to hear the police arrive. So many bullets hit the Benz that it was no longer recognizable.

Pauleena watched as the Jamaicans shot and killed cops with no remorse. Her enemies made it clear that they weren't afraid to die and that they felt as if they were above the law. After about a ten minute shoot out with the cops, finally the Jamaicans began to retreat and flee from the crime scene.

Once the gunfire had stopped, Pauleena and Big Ock were roughly snatched out of the Benz and handcuffed. Men wearing jackets that had the letters F.B.I. written on the back roughly snatched Pauleena up to her feet and rushed her over to the back of an all black sedan. As Pauleena was escorted to the sedan she couldn't help but notice all of the cameramen that had gathered around the scene. It was at that very moment when she knew she had just fucked up.

CHAPTER 36

"Easy Work"

"This what I do!" The Terminator yelled into the camera as he fired away at the punching bag that hung in front of him. Several camera men and press gathered in the gym to watch the champ train for his upcoming fight. "Can't nobody beat me!" he yelled out to no one in particular.

"Omar The Truth Anderson said that this fight won't go pass the fifth round. What do you have to say about that?" a Chinese reporter asked holding his recorder out towards The Terminator.

"Omar is a clown," The Terminator said nonchalantly. "But he's right this fight won't go past five rounds. I plan on getting him out of there real early because I got things to do."

"Omar has one of the best left hooks the sport has seen in a while. How do you plan on dealing with that?" another reporter asked.

"Listen, skills pay the bills around here," The Terminator said as sweat flew with each punch he delivered to the heavy bag. "Besides, we all know Omar's got a glass jaw."

"Omar said he plans on roughing you up in the ring. How do you plan to deal with his rough house tactics?"

"Listen; pound for pound I'm the best!" The Terminator boasted. "Omar is a C-class fighter at best. He's never been in the ring with someone as gifted as me and when we get in the ring I plan to prove that from the opening bell."

The Terminator turned away from the reporters when he heard a female voice call his name. He turned and saw Lisa standing there with a stank look on her face. Lisa and The Terminator had been together for a year and a half and for a year and a half everyday Lisa found herself having to fight off women who were trying to steal her man. She was finding out first hand that being in a relationship with a celebrity wasn't all that it was cracked up to be. Yes, The Terminator was a good man, but he just couldn't help himself when it came to the groupies.

"Hey baby wassup?" The Terminator said with a smile.

"Hey baby my ass!" Lisa snapped. "Why the hell are there so many half naked women walking around in here? Is this a boxing gym or the playboy mansion?"

"Baby don't come up here with all that. I'm just trying to do my job."

"How the fuck can you do your job with all these *distractions* around here?" Lisa asked looking him up and down. She knew her man was training for a big fight, but she had to let her presence be known just in case a bitch tried to get out of pocket with her man.

"So you came all the way to the gym to fuss or did you come to support me?" The Terminator asked.

"Good luck champ," a big-breasted woman in a tight fitting turquoise dress said, as she seemed to appear out of thin air. She then blew him a kiss before walking off.

The Terminator looked over at Lisa and thought he saw smoke coming out of her ears. Thankfully, Mr. Wilson came over right on time.

"Fuck is you over here doing!" Mr. Wilson barked. "You supposed to be training. Why are you over here bullshitting? Omar is training!" he scolded.

"Fuck Omar! I'll beat him with my eyes closed," The Terminator boasted.

"You got all night to talk to Lisa!"

"Baby I'll holla at you when I'm done," The Terminator blew Lisa a kiss. On the outside he had a smile on his face, but on the inside he was pissed that the chick in the turquoise dress had slipped away before he got the chance to bag her.

"Stay focused champ!" Mr. Wilson said in a stern tone. He hated when the public and media came to the open workout sessions. All it did was distract his fighter. Of course he knew it was The Terminator's job to sell the fight, but at the same time it was his job to have his fighter ready when he stepped foot in the ring. "I heard Omar's game plan is to rough you up. He plans to take three punches just to deliver one."

The Terminator shook his head. "When will these fighters learn that I can't be beat?"

"Anybody can be beat! Anybody...," Mr.Wilson growled. "Don't you ever take any fighter lightly because all it takes is one punch to ruin your whole career."

"If Omar beats me, I'll retire from boxing."

Mr. Wilson shook his head. "You know that big house you living in, all those fancy cars you drive, and all of those beautiful women you love to sleep with?"

"Yeah what about it?"

"That's everybody's motivation! They beat you and then they get your life. Don't let one of these motherfuckers steal your life!"

The Terminator hated to admit it but everything that Mr. Wilson had told him was right. It was sad but true that in the game of boxing, all it took was one punch and the public would never look at you the same. "Everything you said just made a lot of sense," The Terminator admitted as he continued to work the heavy bag.

"All I'm saying is, stay focused and stay hungry because it's plenty of people out there that would love to eat your food."

After a long four hour workout The Terminator showered and got dressed in the locker room. While he was alone, Mr. Wilson's words echoed in his head. A lot of people would love to see him lose, but he could care less because as far as he was concerned, he didn't know how to lose. The Terminator stepped out the locker room and was met by a sexy reporter. The reporter wore a nice skirt suit with an expensive pair of heels on her feet.

"Can I finally get a word from you champ before you go?" the reporter asked in a sexy tone.

"Normally I don't do this, but for you I'll make an exception," The Terminator smiled. Just as he was about to go in for the kill, Lisa appeared out of nowhere.

"You ready to go baby?" She made sure she let the word baby roll off of her tongue to let the reporter know that she was the main woman in his life.

"Oh I'm sorry. Am I interrupting something?" the reporter asked.

"As a matter of fact you are," Lisa said rolling her eyes. "I need to feed and fuck my man. Now if you'll excuse us," she said slyly then escorted her man away from the vultures.

"What was that all about back there?" The Terminator asked once his team of security guards made sure that him and Lisa was safely in the back seat of the Escalade.

"I'm tired of all these thirsty ass bitches all in my man's face! Why don't them bitches go find they own man?" Lisa said pouting like a big baby.

"What's with you and all this jealous shit?"

"You would be jealous too if every time you turned around I had a nigga all up in my face!" she told him. "But I would never do that to you because I have too much respect for you to do some shit like that."

"So what are you saying? I don't respect you?" The Terminator asked.

"I ain't saying nothing. You are showing me just how much you respect me." Lisa rolled her eyes.

"A'ight I'mma show you right now," The Terminator said. "Yo driver, pull over!" he ordered. The Escalade slowed down and then finally came to a complete stop. "Get ya shit and get the fuck out!"

Lisa looked at The Terminator to see if he was joking or if he was serious and his eyes said that he wasn't playing. "You just gonna throw me out on the side of the road like I'm a piece of trash?"

The Terminator looked over to his bodyguard. "Get this bitch out of my ride." He sat back and watched as his security roughly snatched Lisa out of the Escalade and toss her out onto the street like she was worthless. Lisa hit the ground hard and before she could look up, the Escalade was gone.

CHAPTER 37

"Bail Money"

Pauleena sat in a holding cell along with several other
women for over fifteen hours. She knew that the cops
were just holding her to fuck with her, but she refused
to let them break her. She sat on the hard bench with her
arms folded in an attempt to keep warm. The police purposely
had the holding cell freezing, but at the moment the cold was
the least of Pauleena's problems. She had more important
things on her mind like what was going to happen when
Chico found out that she had been arrested yet again. From
how bad things were, she was sure that her face was on every
newspaper and news broadcasting station. A gang of
Jamaicans tried to murder her. That was something worth
putting on the front page of a newspaper. Pauleena had no
idea how things would play out from here. All she could do
was hope and pray that things turned out better than how she
anticipated them to. As Pauleena sat on the hard cold bench,
she noticed a big fat ugly chick who had been sleeping on the
hard floor wake up with an attitude.

The fat chick got up, cleared her throat, and hog spit a glob of spit on the wall. She then walked over to the toilet, pulled her pants down, and began to take a loud noisy shit.

Immediately the smell of shit assaulted Pauleena's nostrils. With all the women, being in such a small area there was no way to avoid the smell. They all were forced to just sit there and deal with it.

When the fat chick was done, she got up, pulled her pants up, and walked away as if wiping her ass and flushing the toilet was the furthest thing from her mind.

"Damn you ain't gonna flush that?" a dark skin chick who was sitting next to Pauleena barked.

"Bitch I ain't flushing shit!" the fat chick spat. "As a matter of fact, one of you bitches need to get up so I can sit down cause a bitch sho is tired!" she barked as she looked down the line of women who sat on the bench. The fat chick eyed each woman and stopped when her eyes landed on Pauleena. All of the other women looked rough and were dressed in street attire while Pauleena was dressed in a nice black pants suit. Out of all the women in the holding cell she looked to be the weakest one if one was to judge by the type of clothes one wore.

"Bitch my feet hurt!" the fat chick barked looking down at Pauleena. "Get yo ass up so I can sit down," she growled through clenched teeth.

Pauleena slowly got up and allowed the fat chick to have her seat.

"That's what the fuck I thought," the fat chick said as she sat down on the bench. As soon as her butt hit the bench, Pauleena moved in a blur. Before the fat chick knew what happened, she had been blasted in the face with three punches that forced her head to bounce off the wall. Pauleena grabbed the back of the fat chick's head with both hands and pulled it down as she rammed a hard knee into her face. The fat chick's nose shattered immediately as blood splashed all over the place. Pauleena then grabbed the fat chick by the hair and roughly tossed her down to the floor.

"That's my seat bitch!" Pauleena said as she delivered one last kick to the woman's face before she went back and took her seat on the bench. The rest of the women in the cell stared at Pauleena with nervous looks. Her face was covered in specs of blood and she looked unbothered like nothing had even happened.

Ten minutes later two cops came and got Pauleena and escorted her to a room that had nothing but a table and two chairs inside. She helped herself to a seat and waited patiently. Pauleena already knew how the cops operated. She knew they liked to let people sit for as long as possible hoping they would get scared and crack, but not Pauleena. She had been over the drill more than enough times.

Ten minutes later a man walked in the room wearing a wife-beater and jeans that's slightly hung off his ass. On his feet was a pair of yellow construction Timbs and a Yankee hat sat backwards on his head. "Hello Pauleena."

"Fuck you!" Pauleena countered.

"I'm detective Anthony Stone," he extended his hand. After a few seconds of having his hand hanging he put it down. "Listen, I ain't gonna laugh with you, joke with you, or play with you," he began. "These Jamaican motherfuckers want you dead and honestly there's way too many of them," he chuckled. "I don't know what you did to piss them off, but obviously it's too late to fix it."

"Where's my lawyer?"

"Let me help you," Stone said.

"Help me?" Pauleena laughed. "Nigga please!"

"When you get out of here those Jamaicans are not going to stop until you are dead!" Stone told her. "Let me help you; at least you'll still be alive."

"I'd rather die than live being a rat!"

"A'ight well that's your choice," Stone shrugged. "I could be in the strip club right now so if you don't want my help then that's fine, but just know that I'm going to be the one to slap the cuffs on you if the Jamaicans don't take you out first."

Pauleena was about to say some slick shit when she noticed another detective enter the room.

"She made bail," the detective said. "She's free to go."

Pauleena smiled as she got up and bumped shoulders with Detective Stone on her way out.

"I'll be seeing you soon," Stone said smiling as he looked at Pauleena's ass as she made her exit.

CHAPTER 38

"Guess Who"

Pauleena stepped foot out the jail and was immediately swarmed by the media. Several cameras and microphones were shoved in her face. Two of her bodyguards stood outside waiting for her arrival and quickly made a path to the Escalade that awaited her. When Pauleena hopped in the back seat of the Escalade, she was expecting to see her lawyer Mr. Goldberg sitting there, but to her surprise it was Chico sitting there and the look on his face said that he was pissed.

"I can explain. It wasn't my fault...."

Chico quickly waved her silent with his hand.

After an hour of riding in silence, the Escalade pulled into the clear port where Chico's jet awaited. Pauleena hopped out the Escalade and saw dozens of Columbian men standing around holding A.K.'s. Chico grabbed her by the arm and rushed her toward the jet.

Thoughts of trying to make a run for it crossed Pauleena's mind but with so many of Chico's men around she knew that would be like committing suicide.

Once on the jet, Chico forcefully sat Pauleena in a seat, walked back to the front of the jet, and had a quick word with the captain. He then returned with a glass of tequila in his hand.

"Chico I can explain," Pauleena said. "It's not what it looks..."

Chico's hand shot out in a blur and smacked the shit out of Pauleena while she was in mid-sentence.

Chico downed the rest of his drink in one gulp. "I put my reputation on the line for you and this is what you do?"

Pauleena wanted to reply, but she didn't want to get hit again so he remained silent.

"All I asked you to do was lay low!" he yelled. "To lay low, but I guess that was too much to ask!"

"I'm sorry," Pauleena said in a voice barely above a whisper.

"Your sorry?" Chico growled as he walked over to Pauleena and pulled out his dick and jammed it in her mouth. He grabbed the back of her head with both hands and fucked her mouth a hundred miles per hour. The more Pauleena gagged, the harder Chico pumped.

Just when, Pauleena felt like she was going to throw up, Chico removed his dick from her mouth and roughly removed her pants. Chico couldn't help but smirk when he saw that she didn't have on any panties.

Chico turned Pauleena around facing the seat and forcefully rammed his dick inside of her from the back. He watched as her plump ass bounced off his torso with each stroke he delivered.

Pauleena arched her back and came a long drawn out orgasm. Her moans were never ending. She then got up and flipped Chico over onto her seat. She squatted over him and used the back of the seat for support. Pauleena came up slow, but went down with force. Her skin slapping against his sounded like the ultimate battle. Chico grabbed Pauleena's waist, jerked, and let out a loud groan. Pauleena grabbed Chico's face and gave him a long sloppy kiss.

"I missed you," she whispered.

"I missed you too baby."

CHAPTER 39

"*Frustration*"

Wolf sat in his motel room staring at the TV. He watched the replay of Pauleena getting released from jail over and over again. The more he watched the clip, the more it pissed him off. Ever since Pauleena was released from jail she'd basically disappeared off the face of the earth. No one had seen or heard from her since her release. It seemed as if every channel that Wolf turned to, Pauleena's face was on it. Wolf grabbed the remote, turned the TV off, and closed his eyes. For the past few nights Wolf had tried to drown himself in alcohol to escape from the reality of how fucked up his life was.

His daughter was dead, his fiancé was dead, and most importantly on the inside he was dead. Without his family, he had no purpose to live, no need to live, and no desire to live. All Wolf cared about now was killing Pauleena. He no longer cared about his own life. Jail or death didn't scare him. All that mattered to him was that he made Pauleena pay for what she had did to his family.

Wolf's thoughts were interrupted when he heard a loud banging noise coming from the bathroom. He quickly got up and made his way to the bathroom. In the tub laid a bloody and battered man with his hands taped behind his back and his ankles bounded together. "You ready to talk?" Wolf asked as he roughly snatched the strip of tape from the wounded man's lips.

"I told you already, I don't know where to find Pauleena," the man cried. "I never even met her before. I'm just trying to make a few dollars that's all."

Wolf bent down and punched the man in his mouth. He then rammed the back of the man's head against the back of the tub that caused a huge gash to form in the back of the man's head. Wolf then stood up and removed his .45 from his waistband and aimed it at the man's head. "Last time I'm going to ask you. Where's Pauleena?"

"I told you already man," the man cried. "I don't know."

Wolf stood over the bloodied man and pulled the trigger and watched as his head exploded. He was tired of playing Mr. Nice guy. If he had to kill a million people in order to track Pauleena down, then that's exactly what he was going to do.

CHAPTER 40

"Last Chance"

Pauleena lay naked on Chico's water bed with a glass of wine in her hand. She was still alive because once again Chico had stuck his neck out there for her. Pauleena really liked Chico and was thankful for all that he had done for her. The only problem was moving all the way out to Columbia. Columbia wasn't a place that Pauleena seen herself staying for a long time, but right now she felt like she had no choice but to stay.

Chico walked in his bedroom fully dressed in an expensive tailored suit. He removed his suit jacket and laid it across the bed. He then walked over to the bar area in the bedroom and poured himself a strong drink. "Hola."

"Is daddy still mad at me?" Pauleena flashed an innocent smile.

"Daddy is very mad at you right now," Chico said. "Here's the deal, either you move here with me or you die; simple as that. The choice is yours."

"Baby I want to be with you but…"

"No buts!" Chico said cutting her off. "It's either you stay here with me or you die. The higher ups already want to kill you. I promised them that you would stay with me, but if you decide to leave then you're no longer my problem."

"So if I leave, you are just going to let them kill me?" Pauleena questioned.

"I can't stop them," Chico told her. "You are very reckless and the big bosses hate recklessness because recklessness leads to jail."

"I understand." Pauleena sipped her drink and began to stare blankly out into space. She had a major decision to make, a decision that could cost her, her life. "Okay I'll move with you, but can we please move somewhere more alive?"

"What did you have in mind?"

"Maybe Paris, Brazil, or maybe even Mexico," Pauleena suggested.

"We can move to Paris, but I'll still have to come to Columbia twice a week," Chico compromised. "I think you are making a wonderful decision."

"I know you'll make it worth my while," Pauleena said. She smiled as she got up and slid into Chico's arms. "You really think this can work?"

"What?"

"Me and you," Pauleena said. She loved spending time with Chico not to mention the sex was great, but being in a relationship with him and being in a whole new atmosphere was a totally different story.

"Of course it's going to work because we are going to make it work," Chico said placing a soft kiss on Pauleena's lips. "But I need your word that you're done with all this drug dealing business. We bosses now."

"I promise I'm done," Pauleena promised. "I just need to go back to New York and thank all of my peoples for everything they have ever done for me, not to mention I have to get my money that I have in the safe at my place."

"With me you'll never have to worry about money again," Chico said confidently. "You will be well protected so you never have to carry a gun again. Here no one can hurt you, not The Spades, not the Jamaicans, no one!"

Pauleena smiled. For the first time in her life she had someone that would protect her, someone that would love and take good care of her and it felt great. "You promise you got me?"

"I promise, but I'm going to tell you now, you are going to have to be completely honest with me because without honesty this thing won't work," Chico said in a serious tone.

"Likewise," Pauleena countered. "And while I'm gone that should give you time to get rid of any women that you may have tucked away in the stash."

Chico laughed. "I assure you, you have nothing to worry about. Go handle your business. You got two days."

"What if I don't want to leave right away?" Pauleena seductively licked her lips. "I was thinking maybe I could stay here with you for about a week. Everything else can wait."

"You just read my mind," Chico said as he began to unbuckle his belt.

CHAPTER 41

"Adjustments"

Big Ock sat at the bar area in Pauleena's mansion staring at the security cameras. Ever since the Jamaicans had tried to ambush them, he was determined to be more focused and not get caught slipping again. A part of him wanted to retaliate against the Jamaicans, but that wasn't his call to make. Big Ock downed a shot of Tequila in one gulp, slammed his glass down, and poured himself another shot. Sitting next to Big Ock was his iPhone. He glanced down at his phone every other second hoping to see Pauleena's name flash across the screen. It had been over a week since him and Pauleena were arrested and when he was released, he was told that Pauleena had been taken away by a Columbian man in an expensive suit and he hadn't heard from her since. Big Ock hoped and prayed that Pauleena was okay. He knew that the big shootout with the Jamaicans would make the front page in every city as well as headlines on every station, but it was one thing that Big Ock knew. He knew that whenever Pauleena did go out she would go out with a bang. Without Pauleena on the streets business had pretty much began to dry up. Customers were beginning to complain and threaten to take their business elsewhere, but at the moment there wasn't much that Big Ock could do. If he didn't hear from Pauleena within another week he had already decided that he would take matters into his own hands and become the new face and name of the business.

Big Ock downed another shot. His phone suddenly lit up, he looked down at his screen, and saw that this wasn't a regular call but instead a FaceTime call. Big Ock accepted the call and instantly Pauleena's face appeared on the screen.

"You're alive!" Big Ock said as his face lit up with joy and excitement. To say that he was happy to see and hear from Pauleena was an understatement. "Where are you?"

"I'm in Columbia," Pauleena replied. "Chico came and got me personally."

"Damn," Big Ock shook his head. "You okay?"

"Yeah I'm good, but I'm afraid I have some bad news for you," Pauleena told him. "It looks as if I'm going to have to stay out here in Columbia."

"Are you serious? Fuck you gonna be doing out there?"

Pauleena shrugged. "I have no idea. All I know is that if I don't stay here, I'm going to die," she chuckled. "I'm boxed into a corner."

"We had a good run while it lasted," Big Ock said smiling as he thought back on all the good times and memories that him and Pauleena had shared.

"I'm passing the torch over to you if you want it," Pauleena said. "It's all yours if you want it; the mansion, the clientele, the cars, it's all yours just say the word."

"Think I can handle all that?"

"I know you can," said Pauleena. "I'll be your supplier so I'll make sure you stay with the best quality of drugs."

"So this is it huh? I'm never going to see you again unless I come to Columbia?" Big Ock asked.

Pauleena chuckled. "Of course not. I'll be back at the end of the week to pick up a few things. I can only stay for one night, but while I'm there I'll go over everything with you.

"Sounds good to me," Big Ock said. "How have they been treating you out there?"

"I have no complaints. It is what it is," she smiled. "You just make sure you handle your business up there and be careful. I'll see you at the end of the week," Pauleena said and then ended the call.

Big Ock hung up the phone with a smile on his face. He was happy to hear that Pauleena was doing good and in good spirits, but the icing on the cake was the good news she had just delivered to him. With Pauleena stepping down, that meant that now Big Ock was the man in charge. He was the man running the show and most importantly the man to see. "Ay!" he called out to one of the Muslim bodyguards that stood nearby. "Call up a few people and let them know that I'm the man in charge now and that any business they have with Pauleena, I'll be taking care of it now."

"You got it boss," the bodyguard nodded his head.

"And I'm going to need you to call up a few people and let them know we going to throw a small going away party for Pauleena at the end of the week. Make sure they keep it on the hush because I want it to be a surprise," Big Ock told him.

"You got it boss," the guard said and then went to go do as he was told.

CHAPTER 42

"Fight Night"

Three stretch hummers pulled up back to back in the underground parking area. Immediately several cameras surrounded the vehicles trying to get a glimpse of who was inside. Several huge men filed out of the first Hummer with black shirts on that had the word security written on the back in white letters. The back door to the second Hummer opened and out stepped The Terminator. He was dressed in an all white Armani tailored suit, covering his eyes were a pair of dark designer shades and on his arm was Lisa. She was dressed in an expensive looking white dress that stopped just above her knees. She was still upset at how The Terminator had kicked her out of his car a few weeks back, but since then he had apologized and the two had been working hard on their relationship. Of course The Terminator showed how sorry he was by buying Lisa a diamond bracelet.

The Terminator's team of security escorted him and the rest of his team into the arena and immediately the place was filled with electricity. A cameraman walked backwards in front of the champ wanting to catch his every move and a second camera followed up the rear. As The Terminator headed towards his dressing room, he noticed up ahead that his opponent Omar and a few members of his entourage were standing in front of his dressing room waiting for the champ to arrive.

"Excuse us gentlemen," The Terminator's head security guard a huge man that went by the name Bear said.

"Fuck that!" Omar snapped. "We ain't going nowhere until the champ apologizes for the shit he said about my mother!"

A week ago, The Terminator uploaded a video dissing his opponent and in the video, he made a few slick and tasteless comments about Omar's mother.

"Fuck you and your mother," The Terminator said with a smirk. He knew that would get under the challengers skin.

Omar and his entourage tried to get at The Terminator, but his security held them off. When Omar realized he wouldn't be able to get to The Terminator, he did the next best thing. Omar reached out and grabbed a hand full of Lisa's hair and violently slung her down to the floor where two men from his entourage were able to deliver a few kicks before security was able to separate the two crews.

"This shit ain't over motherfucker! I'll see you in the ring!" Omar yelled as he was escorted away. This was no longer business. It had just become personal.

The Terminator was rushed into his dressing room and immediately the paramedics attended to Lisa's wounds. She had a few nicks and bruises but nothing serious. "I'm going to kill that motherfucker!" The Terminator growled as he quickly removed his suit and replaced that with a pair of red leather trunks with a red pair of custom made boxing shoes to match.

"Calm down," Mr. Wilson said. He knew that Omar had gotten into The Terminator's head and that was a sign of trouble. Boxing was 90% mental and 10% physical and if his fighter's mental wasn't right then, The Terminator was in for a long night. "Stay calm and don't let him get you out of your game plan."

"Fuck the game plan!" The Terminator snapped. "He put his hands on my girl! It's on!"

"Stick to the game plan champ!" Mr. Wilson yelled. "He wants to turn this shit into a brawl and that's not your game."

"I got this," The Terminator said as he sat down and got his hands wrapped.

"Baby I'm okay," Lisa said in an attempt to comfort her man. The last thing she wanted was for The Terminator to get knocked out because his mind wasn't right.

"I'm good baby," The Terminator said in a calm tone. On the outside he looked to be calm, but on the inside he was on fire. The only thing on his mind was punishing Omar for what he had just done. While The Terminator got his hands wrapped, a dark skin lady applied oil to his chest and back and then she began to massage his shoulders.

An hour later, The Terminator stood in the dressing room doing pad work with Mr. Wilson while he went over the game plan one more time with his fighter.

The Terminator seemed regular, but Mr. Wilson could tell that something about him just wasn't right. Several cops peeked their head in the dressing room and announced that it was time for The Terminator to make his way to the ring.

"Let's go champ!" Mr. Wilson said in an attempt to hype his fighter up. The Terminator exited his dressing room and he could feel the floor rumbling underneath him. Fight fans from all across the world gathered in the arena in hopes to see a good fight or better yet to see The Terminator suffer his first defeat.

The sound of Young Jeezy's song "Seen It All" blasting through the speakers informed The Terminator that it was time to head down to the ring. The Terminator's bodyguards had to slap several fight fans hands away as fans tried to kill themselves just to get a touch of the champ. The Terminator entered the room and immediately him and Omar locked eyes and got into an intense stare down. Once the introductions were made, the two fighters met in the middle of the ring where the referee went over the rules.

"Gentlemen I want a nice clean fight!" the referee said sternly. "Both of y'all's trunks are good. When I say break I expect both of you to break cleanly." The referee looked at both fighters. "Touch gloves and let's get it on!" he shouted as the two fighters touched gloves and headed to mutual corners.

"It's show time!" Mr. Wilson yelled. "It's either going to be you or him! Kill or be killed!" he said as he slipped a mouth piece in The Terminator's mouth.

Ding!

Ding!

Ding!

At the sound of the bell, fight fans stood to their feet and began cheering loudly in anticipation of a great fight. Immediately Omar charged towards The Terminator with his guard high. Once he was within striking distance, he fired off a stiff jab followed by a right hook.

The Terminator blocked the jab and ducked the hook with ease.

"Don't run now!" Omar barked as he cut the ring off, boxing The Terminator in a corner. The Terminator landed a quick left hook to the side of Omar's ear and quickly used his legs to get out of the corner.

"Get back!" The Terminator said as he delivered a stiff jab that bounced off of Omar's forehead. Omar ate the jab and moved into a good position to land a punch, but The Terminator quickly clinched and grabbed both of Omar's arms so he wouldn't be able to fire off a punch.

"Stop holding me like a little bitch!" Omar barked as the referee separated the two. Omar then quickly rushed The Terminator back into the corner and fired off a straight right hand followed by a powerful hook. The Terminator leaned against the ropes and sunk into his Philly shell defense; the same defense that Floyd Money Mayweather had made famous.

The first punch The Terminator blocked with his glove, while the other punch bounced off his shoulder. Omar went to throw another punch, but The Terminator landed a quick counter right upper cut that lifted his head up and then he was gone before Omar's next punch even had a chance of landing. The Terminator flashed a smile and then landed a jab in the center of Omar's face forcing his head to snap back. Omar quickly bull rushed The Terminator back into the ropes and fired off a five punch combination directed at The Terminator's body. The Terminator quickly grabbed Omar in a clench, but just as the referee was about to break them up, Omar snuck in an uppercut that stunned The Terminator. Immediately The Terminator threw a left hook followed by a right hook. Omar took the punches well as he to fired off two hooks of his own that landed on the side of The Terminator's head. The two then proceeded to go blow for blow until the bell sounded and the referee quickly jumped in between the two men.

"Let's get it!" Omar yelled in The Terminator's face before he headed back to his corner.

As soon as The Terminator hit the corner, Mr. Wilson was all over him. "What the fuck are you doing!" he yelled as he splashed water in The Terminator's face. "This is an easy fight son! Don't make it difficult! Stick to the game plan! Box this guy! Don't turn this into a slug fest!"

Ding!

Ding!

Ding!

The two met in the middle of the ring and The Terminator quickly landed a quick jab that snapped Omar's head back. He followed up with a hook that if it would have connected, it would have knocked Omar's head clean off. Omar ducked the hook and came back with a monster uppercut that landed under The Terminator's chin. The punch stunned The Terminator. His legs immediately turned into noodles as he tried to hold on to Omar for dear life. Omar roughly pushed The Terminator off of him and unloaded a ten punch combination until The Terminator finally hit the canvas. The crowd erupted in a loud roar when they saw The Terminator struggling to get back up to his feet.

"Shit!" The Terminator said to himself. This was the first time he had ever hit the deck in his entire career. He looked out into the crowd and saw all the fans cheering because he had been dropped. He and Mr. Wilson had been over what to do if he ever got dropped in the ring over a hundred times in the gym, but it was different now that it was actually happening. The Terminator wobbled back up to his feet and took a deep breath.

"Five!... Six!... Seven!... Eight!..." the referee yelled loudly in The Terminator's face. "Are you okay!?"

"Yeah I'm good!"

"Walk to me!" the referee instructed. The crowd was so loud that he basically had to yell at the top of his lungs just so The Terminator could hear him. "Okay let's get it on!"

Once The Terminator made it back to his feet, Omar came in and tried to finish the champ off. He bull rushed The Terminator back into the ropes and fired off several powerful punches. The Terminator rested against the ropes with his guard held high. He blocked most of the punches, but a few managed to slip through. The bell sounded off and the referee quickly separated the two men.

Once The Terminator made it, back to the corner Mr. Wilson was all over him. "Keep your fucking hands up!" He snatched the mouthpiece from The Terminator's mouth. "Why are you fighting his fight? Be smart and use your head! Don't exchange with him!"

The Terminator nodded his head. He was more embarrassed than hurt. Millions of fans all across the world had just witnessed him getting knocked down. His ego was hurt more than his physical.

Ding!

Ding!

Ding!

The bell sounded and immediately The Terminator was eager to get revenge on Omar for embarrassing him in front of the entire world. He started out with a double jab that bounced off of Omar's face. He faked with the jab, but instead threw a sweeping right hook. Omar saw the punch coming, but wasn't quick enough to avoid the blow. The punch landed clean on his chin. The crowed ooo'd and ahhhh'd but Omar took the punch well and kept on coming forward.

"Get back!" The Terminator yelled as he snapped Omar's head back with his jab. Omar lunged forward with a wide left hook, but The Terminator blocked the punch with his shoulder and countered with a quick right hook that bounced off the side of Omar's head. Omar went to fire off another punch, but The Terminator was gone.

"Fight me man to man and stop running!" Omar growled. He wanted so badly to hurt the champ that he was even willing to hurt himself in the process.

The Terminator faked high and low landing a stiff jab in the pit of Omar's stomach.

"Fuck this!" Omar said as he rushed The Terminator back into the ropes, but before he could get a punch off, The Terminator quickly tied him up. Just as the referee broke the two men apart the bell sounded off signaling the end of the round.

"That's what the fuck I'm talking about!" Mr. Wilson yelled as soon as The Terminator made it back to the corner. "Use your speed and you got this in the bag!" He squirted a mouthful of water in The Terminator's mouth. "Listen champ, he can't take it downstairs. Attack that body and watch his hands start to come down." He slipped the mouth piece back in The Terminator's mouth and watched him head to the middle of the ring for the start of round four.

Immediately The Terminator threw a jab followed by a hook to the stomach that caused Omar to double over. Just like Mr. Wilson predicted Omar slightly lowered his hands in an attempt to protect his stomach. The Terminator got close up on Omar and landed two more hooks to the body and in return he received a hook that he partially blocked. The Terminator faked like he was about to go low and when he saw Omar drop his hands he landed a straight right hand. The punch staggered Omar and immediately the crowd erupted in a loud roar. The Terminator ran up on Omar and fired off a lightning fast eight punch combination. Each punch landed flush and left Omar dazed. The Terminator landed punch after punch on Omar's exposed face until the referee finally stepped in and stopped the fight. The Terminator's team along with the media and promoters flooded the ring and praised The Terminator.

A commentator smiled as he got ready to question the champ. "So champ you went down early in the fight for the first time but you bounced back. Was this your toughest fight?"

The Terminator looked at the commentator like he was crazy. "Absolutely not! This was an easy fight. Once I started listening to my trainer and sitting on my punches, I knew he was done."

"What about the punch that dropped you in the second round?" the commentator asked.

The Terminator laughed. "Listen, I had to make it believable you know," he said looking directly into the camera. "Had to let the fans get their money's worth."

"Who would you like next?"

"I don't know," The Terminator smiled. "Right now I just want to relax, go to the strip club, and enjoy myself," he said then exited the ring and headed back towards his dressing room.

The Terminator and his team celebrated in the dressing room like they had just won the championship.

"Where we headed tonight champ?" Bear asked with excitement on his face.

"I heard my girl Pauleena supposed to be having a surprise going away party at her mansion tonight," he smiled.

"You know I have to pay my respects and say my last good bye."

CHAPTER 43

"It's Time"

Live Wire sat on the couch and watched Sparkle dance around the house cleaning up as Pharrell's song "Happy" bumped through the speakers. He'd noticed that ever since he and Sparkle had got back together she had been in good spirits and seemed to be genuinely happy. Live Wire also noticed that Sparkle had been doing her best to become a better woman and he appreciated her effort.

"Come dance with me," Sparkle said grabbing Live Wire's hands and tried to pull him up from off the couch, but he refused.

"Not right now baby," Live Wire smiled. He wasn't much of a dancer, but it seemed like the more he refused, the more Sparkle egged him on until finally he gave in. Live Wire and Sparkle stood in the middle of the living room doing the Carlton Banks from "The Fresh Prince of Bel-Air" dance when they heard the doorbell ring.

Live Wire grabbed his .45 off the coffee table as he made his way over to the door. He lived in the suburbs, but after what had happened to Nikki, he wasn't willing to take any chances. He looked through the peephole and slid the gun down in the small of his back, opened the door, and stepped to the side so Wolf could enter.

Wolf walked in and gave Live Wire dap and then he gave Sparkle a hug followed by a kiss on the cheek. "Hey Sparkle how you been?"

"I've been good," Sparkle smiled. "I hope you didn't come over here to get my soon to be husband in no trouble," she said flashing the huge rock that rested on her ring finger.

"Congratulations!" Wolf smiled as he examined the rock. He looked in Sparkle's eyes and all he could see was happiness. Wolf's whole purpose for stopping by was because he had just heard from a Spades member that Pauleena was having a going away party tonight and he wanted to see if Live Wire wanted to join him. He knew how Live Wire had felt about Pauleena and he wanted to see if he wanted in on the action, but after seeing the happiness in Sparkle's eyes he figured that telling Live Wire about the party wasn't such a good idea after all. Wolf knew that there was only a 50/50 chance that he would make it back alive and he thought about how he felt when he found out that Ivy had been killed and he didn't want to put Sparkle through that kind of pain. In his line of work it was hard to find true happiness and it wasn't right for him to do that to Sparkle and Live Wire.

"Imma go upstairs so y'all can talk," Sparkle said and then she quickly disappeared upstairs.

"What's good bro? You found out where that bitch Pauleena hiding yet?"

"Nah not yet," Wolf lied. "I just came by to see how you were holding up."

"You know a few bullets can't stop me," Live Wire boasted. He walked over to the cabinet and pulled out a bottle of Tequila and poured himself and Wolf a shot. "Talk to me. I can tell that something is on your mind."

"I'm good," Wolf lied. He wanted so badly to tell Live Wire about Pauleena's party tonight, but decided it would be best to just keep the info to himself and not get Live Wire in the middle of his mess. He knew that once Live Wire found out that he didn't tell him about the party he would be mad, but at least he would still be alive.

"Something is on your mind. Talk to me bro," Live Wire pressed. He and Wolf had been friends for a long time so it was safe to say that he knew when something wasn't right with his friend.

"Just been thinking about Ivy," Wolf lied. "I miss her." In all reality he was doing his best to not think about Ivy. Losing her was like losing a piece of himself.

"Don't even worry about that. We going to make Pauleena pay for what she did," Live Wire assured him.

"I got a few things I have to take care of. I just wanted to stop by and check on you to make sure you were okay." Wolf stood to his feet, smiled, and gave Live Wire a strong hug. It was the type of hug that someone gave a person when they knew they would never see them again.

"If you need me for anything, you make sure you call me," Live Wire told him. Wolf poured himself one last shot and downed it in one gulp.

"You already know," he said and like that he was gone.

****

Later on that night Wolf stood in the basement dressed in all black with a tech-9 in his hand and an angry look on his face. In front of him stood thirty Spades members that were willing to risk their lives to help Wolf get rid of Pauleena once and for all. Wolf raised his hand and got everyone's attention. "Tonight is the night that we settle this once and for all. All the work we put in over the years was all for tonight," he said. "We take down Pauleena and we will take 85% of the drugs off the streets in New York." Wolf looked down at the gun in his hands. "This is no longer business; it's been personal for me for a long time now. I've lost my fiancé and most importantly, I lost my daughter." He paused as a tear ran down his cheek. "If anybody wants to walk out this door, now is the time because I can promise you that tonight almost none of us will be making it back alive. So if anybody is not built for this, please leave now and I promise you won't be looked at differently. I know a lot of you have families so if you want to leave, now is the time." Wolf paused and waited to see who would leave. Not one man in the basement budged.

Dre stepped up and spoke for every man in the basement. "If they killed your fiancé and your daughter, they might as well had killed all of our wives and kids too!" He was the second in charge and looked up to Wolf sort of like a big brother.

Wolf wiped the tears from his eyes and smiled. To have such a loyal team that would go to bat for him even when they knew that the chances of them returning were slim to none was a wonderful feeling and Wolf couldn't express just how much that meant to him.

"Let's go kill this bitch once and for all!" Wolf said and instantly the basement erupted in a loud roar of cheers. "It's time to go to war!"

CHAPTER 44

"Party Time"

Three all black Escalades stood parked back to back. Big Ock stood leaning up against the first Escalade with a smirk on his face. Tonight was going to be a night that Pauleena would never forget. He had planned the biggest and most wonderful party for his boss. Big Ock wanted to send Pauleena off the right way. Over the years she had done a lot for him and all he wanted to do was return the favor. He knew that Pauleena would be against having such a big party so he kept it a secret. At the mansion were a few people that Pauleena did business with, a few friends, strippers, pimps, hoes, stick up kids, low level hustlers, and a few celebrities. Big Ock had them all to park in the back of the house in the huge back yard so Pauleena wouldn't be alerted when they made it home. The whole time Pauleena had been gone, Big Ock had been preparing to take her place. He was honored that she had trusted him enough to pass the torch on to him. Big Ock was feeling real proud at the moment and tonight he planned on paying Pauleena back with a party that she wouldn't soon forget.

Pauleena stepped foot off the jet like she ran the entire world. She wore a red tight fitting dress that barely covered her ass and on her feet were a pair of red pumps that cost over $1,200.00. A pair of oversized designer shades covered her eyes and her hair hung down her back and bounced with every step that she took. Pauleena made her way towards the Escalades while two Columbian men with no nonsense looks on their faces brought up the rear. Chico had given Pauleena specific instructions. Go to her house, get what she needed, say bye to who she needed to, and come straight back to Columbia. After hearing about the drama that Pauleena had with the Jamaicans, Chico sent two of his best soldier to go back to America with Pauleena to make sure that she made it back it him in one piece. The soldiers he sent were two of the baddest men Columbia had ever seen. The first man was a short stocky man that went by the name Hector. Hector was known for being one of the most feared men in the world. The second man was much taller. He stood 6"7 tall and went by the name Macho. Macho had a long scar on his face and had been one of Chico's best soldiers for years.

Pauleena walked up and hugged Big Ock. "Good to see you again," she joked.

"I thought you were never coming back," Big Ock smiled.

"Tonight is my last night in New York," she said sadly. "I'm officially moving to Columbia tonight."

"Tonight?" Big Ock asked. "What you mean tonight? You just got here."

"The higher ups want my head on a stick so I'm not really in no position to make a fuss about anything," Pauleena told him as they all boarded the Escalade.

"But I'm saying though, you just got here. You can't leave in the morning?" Big Ock pressed. The surprise party he had planned was sure to last until the morning.

"Chico wants me back in Columbia as soon as possible," Pauleena said and then poured herself a glass of champagne from the open bottle that rested in a bucket of ice. "After my run in with the Jamaicans, he's a little worried about my safety."

"I see," Big Ock said with his gaze falling on the two Columbian men that rode in the Escalade with them.

"Columbia's finest," Pauleena said as she sipped her champagne. A part of her didn't want to leave New York or the business that took so much to build, but at the moment she didn't really have that much of a choice. Chico had already expressed to her how the higher ups were sick and tired of her shenanigans and he could no longer protect her from their wrath.

"You cool with all this?"

"I don't really have too much of a choice," Pauleena shrugged. "It's either this or die and I choose this."

"Fuck it! I say we just enjoy the night and worry about everything else later."

****

Wolf sat in an all black van that was parked about two blocks away from Pauleena's mansion. In his hands he held a pair of binoculars. He had been staked out there for the last two hours. Wolf had noticed several fancy cars pull into the back section of the house. The information about the surprise party had been accurate and now all he had to do was wait patiently until Pauleena showed up. "Everybody stay on point. She should be arriving real soon," he told the troops.

Wolf's palms were damp from anticipation on what was about to happen.

"Is Pauleena the only target?" Dre asked.

"No!" Wolf gave Dre a serious look. "We killing everybody in the house!" Just as the words left Wolf's lips, the driver of the van got his attention. "Looks like the package has arrived," he said with a smile.

Wolf adjusted his binoculars and watched three Escalades pull up onto the property back to back and seconds later he saw Pauleena step out the back door of an S.U.V. Just the site of her made Wolf's skin crawl. "Get ready men it's almost time!"

CHAPTER 45

"The Mansion"

"**I**'m sure going to miss this place," Pauleena said as the Escalade pulled onto the estate. "You make sure you take care of my baby while I'm gone," she said looking over at Big Ock.

"Trust me she's in good hands," Big Ock smiled as he slid out the Escalade and held the back door open so Pauleena could exit. Hector and Macho made sure they stood close by Pauleena. If anything was to happen to her, Chico was sure to have both of their asses for breakfast.

"Come on let me get my shit so we can go," Pauleena said and headed towards the front door. She entered through the front door and immediately her hand went to her purse when she saw a house full of people all standing there. Before she could even get a word out everyone in the house yelled.

"SURPRISE!"

Immediately Pauleena turned to Big Ock. "What the fuck is going on!?"

"It's a surprise party," he said smiling. "I figured since this was your last night here I would send you off the right way."

"Are you crazy!" Pauleena yelled in his face. "All these motherfuckers here are sure to draw the attention of the cops. The F.B.I. is probably outside watching us right now!"

"Sorry," Big Ock said with his head hung low. "I was just trying to send you off the right way."

Before Pauleena could say another word, the DJ yelled into his microphone. "Shout out to my girl Pauleena! Let's send her out the right way!" instantly Mack Wilds song "Own it" bumped through the speakers. The music seemed to get everyone hype as everyone seemed to start dancing and celebrating.

Pauleena looked over at Big Ock and rolled her eyes. They were supposed to be moving under the radar and this idiot decided he wanted to throw a big ass house party. Pauleena moved through the crowd with Hector and Macho close on her heels. Both men already had their guns drawn. Macho quickly made a path so Pauleena could walk through. After pushing her way through the crowd, Pauleena finally made it upstairs where she quickly began to grab the few things that she needed. She knew nothing good would come from a party like this; nothing. Pauleena cracked open her safe and began to stuff stacks of money into a pillow case when she heard the familiar sound of gunfire over the intercom.

"What the fuck?" Pauleena said to herself as she walked over to the outside balcony in her bedroom. She stepped foot out on the balcony and saw several men dressed in all black running through the front of her estate carrying guns. She saw several of her Muslim guards sprawled out on the grass. "Shit!" she cursed when she saw the men dressed in all black

enter through the front door. Pauleena quickly walked over to her gun closet, snatched the door open, and pulled out an Uzi and prepared for battle.

****

On a silent count of three, Dre shot the locks off the front door and watched as all The Spades ran up in there and opened fire on anything moving. He and Wolf were the last to enter the mansion. Wolf watched as people ran all throughout the mansion for a place to hide, but The Spades took them all down one by one.

Big Ock jetted upstairs and escaped several bullets by an inch or two. Once everyone was dead, Wolf, Dre, and rest of The Spades slowly made their way upstairs. They knew Pauleena was in the mansion somewhere and it was their job to find her. They were headed down a long hallway with doors lined up on each side. When out of nowhere a door opened and Pauleena stuck her arms out the door and pulled the trigger on her Uzi swaying her arms back and forth. Several Spades dropped like dominoes before Wolf and a few others returned fire.

Suddenly another room door opened from the opposite side the hallway and a stocky Columbian man exited the room holding an A.K. 47. Wolf watched as the Columbian dropped several Spades before he finally fired two shots into the big man's chest. The bullets barely moved the Columbian man. Wolf quickly took cover behind a wall as several A.K. bullets tore through the wall just above Wolf's head.

Dre sprang from behind a wall and opened fire on the big man. The shells from his shotgun ripped Hector in half. Behind Dre, Big Ock emerged from a room with a smirk on his face. He aimed his Mac-11 at Dre's back and squeezed down on the trigger. The gun violently rattled in his hands as he watched the bullets spin Dre around. His body shook like a puppet on a string and then he finally collapsed to the marbled floor.

Wolf crept up on Big Ock from behind and blew his brains all over the wall. He had been waiting for a long time to do that and to say that it wasn't satisfying would be a lie. Wolf made his way over to Dre's body and kneeled down. Wolf knew he was dead, but he still checked his pulse anyway. He watched as a few Spades members entered the room that Pauleena was last seen in.

Instantly the sound of several different guns could be heard blasting in a rapid succession. Wolf quickly crept up to the room door and peeked in. To his surprise he had a clear shot at Pauleena. Without thinking twice Wolf sprang inside the room and opened fire. He waved his arms from left to right. One of his bullets hit Pauleena. The impact from the shot spun her around and tossed her over the desk that rested over in the corner. Wolf then quickly turned his gun on the tall man that stood over on the other side of the room. He fired one last shot before he heard a clicking sound that informed him that he was out of bullets. The one shot that he got off knocked the gun out of the big man's hands.

Wolf quickly pulled out his back up weapon, but before he got a chance to use it, Macho rushed him with a hunting knife in his hand. He swiped at Wolf's wrist causing him to drop his gun.

"Come on motherfucker!" Macho barked as he jabbed at Wolf with the knife. Wolf quickly took a few steps back and removed his shirt. He held the shirt like it was a pair of nunchucks. Macho swung the knife at Wolf's stomach and he quickly jumped back out of the way. Macho jabbed the knife towards Wolf's chest. Wolf countered and wrapped his shirt around Macho's wrist with the knife. He then landed a hard left hook that bounced off the side of Macho's head and then he bent Macho's wrist so far back that it threatened to snap. Macho dropped the knife and wrapped his hands around Wolf throat and tried to choke the life out of him. Wolf kneed Macho in the groan. From there the two men stood toe to toe and went blow for blow.

Pauleena looked up from the floor and saw Wolf and Macho getting busy. She looked down and saw a small hole in her thigh and blood everywhere. "Fuck!" she cursed as she slowly climbed back up to her feet. She hopped over to the body of one of The Spades that she had killed and picked up his gun from off the floor and fired a shot up into the ceiling.

"POW!"

The sound of the gun being fired put a stop to both men's fighting.

"Put your fucking hands up!" Pauleena yelled. Wolf just stood there and looked at her with fire dancing in his eyes.

"Kill me bitch!" Wolf growled.

"You couldn't let it go could you?" Pauleena shook her head. "Just had to keep it going?"

"You killed my family!"

"Fuck your family!" Pauleena said coldly. "You tried to fuck with my money and everybody knows that's the ultimate no, no!"

"Kill this motherfucker so we can get out of here before the cops show up," Macho said.

"You shot me," Pauleena chuckled as she looked down at her leg.

"Kill me!" Wolf growled. He had already lost everything and without Ivy and Little Sunshine, he saw no need for him to continue to live. "Kill me!" he repeated. "Do it!" he banged on his chest.

Pauleena raised her gun at Wolf's head. "Good bye Wolf!"

POW!

Pauleena watched as Wolf's lifeless body crumbled down to the floor and landed in an awkward position. She let out a loud long sigh, dropped her gun, and then limped out onto the balcony. At the moment she needed some air. Pauleena leaned on the rail on the balcony and looked up into the sky. "What a motherfucking day," she said out loud to no one in particular. Pauleena had never pictured her night to end like this. The sound of Pauleena's cell phone ringing snapped her out of her thoughts. She quickly limped back into the room and grabbed her phone. She saw Chico's name flashing across the screen. "Hey baby," she answered and then limped back out onto the balcony.

"Hey what's going on?" Chico asked.

"I've been shot baby," Pauleena told him. "Remember The Spades, that organization I was telling you about? Well they showed up and tried to kill me tonight."

"Did they?" Chico asked in a dry non-interested tone.

"Yes baby, but don't worry I did what I had to do so now I can come home," Pauleena said with an exhausted look on her face.

"What home?"

"Huh?" Pauleena said confused.

"You no longer have a home Pauleena," Chico said bluntly.

"What are you talking about baby?"

"You are too much of a loose cannon Pauleena." Chico paused for a second. "You could have had it all, but you are too stubborn and too hot headed."

"Baby please don't do this to me. I have nowhere else to go," Pauleena pleaded. "I did everything you asked of me."

"I asked you to lay low and stay off the radar, but I guess that was too much to ask from a stupid street bitch like you," Chico's voice was suddenly really cold. "Say goodnight Pauleena!" Chico said then the line went dead.

"Hello, hello...." Pauleena said into the phone. She quickly spun around when she heard footsteps coming from behind her.

Macho stood in front of her with a shotgun pointed at Pauleena's head. "Good night Pauleena!" He said then pulled the trigger.

KABOOM!

The shot hit Pauleena in the upper part of her chest. The impact from the blast flipped her body over the balcony. Her body sailed through the air in what seemed like slow motion and then finally her body violent smacked off the concrete. Pauleena's body lay sprawled across the ground in an awkward position as her eyes stared up into the sky.

Macho leaned over the balcony and fired eight more shots into Pauleena's body just to make sure she was dead. "Stupid ass bitch!" he growled as he dropped the gun down to the floor and made his exit as the sound of sirens filled the air.

"Two Days Later"

Live Wire sat in the crib watching the news. For the last two days all the media had been reporting was about the deaths of both Wolf and Pauleena. *"Fuck!"* Live Wire cursed to himself. He knew that if he would have gone with Wolf, that the outcome would have been much different.

"Baby you alright?" Sparkle asked as she noticed that Live Wire was crying. This was the first time she had ever saw him cry and the site of her man crying made her cry.

"Fuck you crying for?" Live Wire asked when he saw the tears streaming down Sparkle's face.

"Nothing," she wiped her face. "I'd just never seen tears from a hustler before," she said as she held Live Wire tightly and did her best to comfort him.

THE END

To contact Silk White: SilkWhite212@yahoo.com

Books by Good2Go Authors on Our Bookshelf

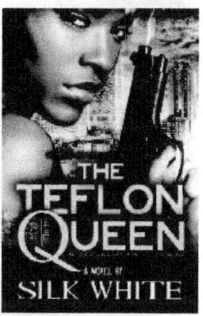

Good2Go Films Presents

To order books, please fill out the order form below:
To order films please go to www.good2gofilms.com

Name: _____
Address: _____
City: _____ State: _____ Zip Code: _____
Phone: _____
Email: _____
Method of Payment: ☐ Check   ☐ VISA   ☐ MASTERCARD
Credit Card#: _____
Name as it appears on card: _____
Signature: _____

Item Name	Price	Qty	Amount
He Loves Me, He Loves You Not - Mychea	$14.99		
He Loves Me, He Loves You Not 2 - Mychea	$14.99		
He Loves Me, He Loves You Not 3 - Mychea	$14.99		
Married To Da Streets – Silk White	$14.99		
My Boyfriend's Wife - Mychea	$14.99		
Never Be The Same – Silk White	$14.99		
Stranded – Silk White	$14.99		
Slumped – Jason Brent	$14.99		
Tears of a Hustler - Silk White	$14.99		
Tears of a Hustler 2 - Silk White	$14.99		
Tears of a Hustler 3 - Silk White	$14.99		
Tears of a Hustler 4- Silk White	$14.99		
Tears of a Hustler 5 – Silk White	$14.99		
Tears of a Hustler 6 – Silk White	$14.99		
The Panty Ripper - Reality Way	$14.99		
The Teflon Queen – Silk White	$14.99		
The Teflon Queen 2 – Silk White	$14.99		
The Teflon Queen – 3 – Silk White	$14.99		
Time Is Money - Silk White	$14.99		
Young Goonz – Reality Way	$14.99		
Subtotal:			
Tax:			
Shipping (Free) U.S. Media Mail:			
Total:			

Make Checks Payable To:
Good2Go Publishing
7311 W Glass Lane
Laveen, AZ 85339

CPSIA information can be obtained
at www.ICGtesting.com
Printed in the USA
LVOW04*1502070416

482603LV00014B/132/P